He *had* to go!

He had to go right now, or things would escalate and he'd lose this woman altogether. And, although he couldn't really understand it, he knew he couldn't let that happen.

Will was trying to untangle himself not only from Alex but from the sheets.

Her hand touched his hip.

'Stay?'

Nothing more than a sibilant whisper, but now Alex was sitting up, sitting behind him, her arms around his chest, her fingers brushing against his nipples in such a way that he almost groaned with agony.

'Help me?'

The words were pressed against his shoulder and, given his condition, there was no way he should have agreed.

But somehow they were lying down again.

He looked into the beseeching blue eyes and knew he was lost. 'Are you sure?' he asked.

She nodded, then reached up to trace his lips with a fingertip.

'Just show me how, Superman,' she whispered.

Dear Reader,

The idea for this book came when I was on a short writing retreat with a group of fellow writers who have been going away—as many as can get together—once a year for about nine years now.

We work in the morning, walk the beach—brave ones swim—usually lunch together, and then have brainstorming sessions or discussions on topics we've already decided on over lunch and into mid-afternoon. We break into smaller groups, or go off on our own, until 'wine o'clock', when we once again get together. These sessions are usually the most productive in producing ideas. Often they're wild ideas—but even wild ideas can be tamed and brought together in a book.

Such is the way of some books, and it took nine months' gestation before this one finally came together in its current form—so I hope this particular baby is as good as the making of it was.

Meredith Webber

THE ONE MAN
TO HEAL HER

BY
MEREDITH WEBBER

First published in Great Britain 2015
by Mills & Boon, an imprint of Harlequin (UK) Limited,
Eton House, 18-24 Paradise Road, Richmond, Surrey, TW9 1SR

© 2015 Meredith Webber

ISBN: 978-0-263-25805-9

Harlequin (UK) Limited's policy is to use papers that are natural,
renewable and recyclable products and made from wood grown in
sustainable forests. The logging and manufacturing processes conform
to the legal environmental regulations of the country of origin.

Printed and bound in Great Britain
by CPI Antony Rowe, Chippenham, Wiltshire

Meredith Webber says of herself, 'Once I read an article which suggested that Mills & Boon® were looking for new Medical Romance™ authors. I had one of those "I can do that" moments, and gave it a try. What began as a challenge has become an obsession—though I do temper the "butt on seat" career of writing with dirty but healthy outdoor pursuits, fossicking through the Australian Outback in search of gold or opals. Having had some success in all of these endeavours, I now consider I've found the perfect lifestyle.'

Books by Meredith Webber

The Accidental Daddy
Date with a Surgeon Prince
One Baby Step at a Time
Christmas Where She Belongs
The Sheikh and the Surrogate Mum
New Doc in Town
Orphan Under the Christmas Tree
Melting the Argentine Doctor's Heart
Taming Dr Tempest

**Visit the author profile page
at millsandboon.co.uk for more titles**

For all the Maytoners, who keep me going.

PROLOGUE

ALEX SAT HUDDLED on a red plastic chair against the wall of the ER room. A woman doctor she vaguely recognised had come towards her earlier but had whisked away when a rush of ambulance cases had been brought in, and now, two hours later, Alex still sat, a little more hunched over, exhaustion having caused her to nod off so several times she'd nearly fallen off the chair.

Twice a male nurse had approached, but, unable to stand the thought of a man touching her, she'd shrunk back and lied, saying she was waiting for someone.

Then the woman doctor she'd seen earlier must have cleared the urgent patients and approached once again.

'Are you here for treatment?' she asked gently.

Alex nodded, not sure she would be able to speak, let alone move, so thick was the cloud of despair and unhappiness that enveloped her.

The doctor knelt and reached out to touch Alex's cheek, brushing at the tears that kept dripping out of her eyes no matter how hard she tried to stop them.

She wondered what the doctor would make of her pathetic behaviour. Probably assume she was a street kid, although would a street kid be wearing clean clothes?

'Can you tell me what's wrong?'

The question focussed Alex's mind.

'I'm bleeding.'

She whispered the words, and heard the huskiness of fear and shame in them—saw the doctor's look of shock—wondered what the doctor would think…

'I'm Dr Isobel Armitage,' the woman said gently. 'Come with me and I'll see what I can do to help you.'

She took Alex's hand, pressed her fingers reassuringly, and led her to a cubicle, pausing only to draw the curtains around it.

The male nurse who'd offered assistance earlier eased through the gap in the curtains. The doctor must have felt Alex cringe and try to hide behind her because she turned and hugged her tightly, asking the nurse to leave them.

'She wouldn't talk to me earlier,' he complained, but the woman called Isobel just shooed him away.

'Are you feeling well enough to tell me who you are? Answer a few questions?'

Alex nodded, and somehow managed to supply her name, Alexandra Hudson, and age, sixteen, but when she came to an address the courage that had shored her up to actually get to the hospital deserted her and she burst into tears.

Once again the doctor held her while she cried, then poked her head outside the door to ask some unseen person to bring in tea with plenty of sugar.

'A hot drink will do you good,' Isobel said, passing the box of tissues to Alex before wrapping a blood-pressure cuff around her arm. Isobel talked as she worked, making notes on a chart that still had no address on it.

The talking helped so by the time the tea arrived the tears had stopped, although the doctor—Isobel—waited until Alex finished her tea before asking quietly, 'Can you tell me what happened?'

Alex lifted her head, knowing she had to be looking

at Isobel as she spoke although cringingly aware of how rough she must look with a tear-streaked face and tangled hair, her clothes thrown on any old how.

Deep breath!

You can do this!

And she did—or she began…

'It was Mr Spencer—Dad's friend. He—he…'

'He raped you?'

Alex nodded.

'I need to examine you,' Isobel told her.

The words were gentle but Alex could see the woman's anger flashing in her eyes. How much of this kind of thing—of men's violence towards woman—had she seen in her job?

'Did you tell your parents?'

Alex knew the question was the obvious one and the doctor had to ask it, but—

The pain of their reaction speared through her yet again, but she had to tell—to explain…

The words came tumbling out in a shivery kind of whisper, forced past the hurt—the rejection…

'They called me a liar and a slut and told me I was no longer their daughter. They're religious, you see. Mr Spencer, he preaches in the church sometimes and I told Mum weeks ago that he kept touching me and she sent me to my room for talking filth.'

Now she was crying again—tears rolling down her cheeks—like a big sook.

She had no idea what the doctor was thinking until she took both of Alex's hands in hers, gently squeezed her fingers once again, and said quietly, 'We should report it to the police.'

Alex nodded. She'd already thought about this and

knew the doctor was right, although the woman looked very surprised by her agreement.

'There's other kids there, at the church, younger than me,' she explained, 'and he touches them too. He shouldn't be allowed—someone has to stop him.'

'You're something special,' Isobel said, smiling at Alex, 'but there's your family to consider as well. There'll be publicity, a court case—how will they handle it?'

Alex shrugged.

'They've kicked me out, what more can they do to me?'

And something in her determination must have come through in the words—the hint of the growing strength that she knew lay beneath her unhappiness—because Isobel reached around her and gave her another a warm hug.

'We'll look after you,' she promised. 'And I'll stand by you all through it. But first…'

She stopped, obviously thinking of the next step.

'I have to phone someone from the police. A woman called Marcie Clarke. She's kind and understanding and has done this kind of police business before,' Isobel told Alex. 'When she gets here we can examine you and take samples.'

'Samples?'

The word fluttered from Alex's lips and Isobel frowned.

'It hasn't just happened? You've been home?'

'I *had* to go home,' Alex told her, the experience coming back to her in all its horror. 'I had to clean myself up and scrub away what that man had done to me, but it was two days ago and there's still blood and I don't know what to do.'

She broke down completely, crying giving way to desolate sobs, then the doctor's arms were around her again, comforting and soothing, shushing and promising that everything would be all right.

Three hours later, the rape reported, Alex comforted by the information that a torn hymen could bleed for a couple of days, and Marcie in charge of what little, probably useless, evidence Isobel had managed to retrieve, the kind doctor who'd got her through the ordeal disappeared to take a phone call.

Alex was exhausted, too tired to even care about what would happen next—where she'd find a bed, how she'd live. Did Heritage Port have places for homeless teenagers?

It was all too much, so she curled up on the narrow bed in the cubicle and fell asleep.

At some time someone must have come in and put a light cover over her because when Isobel woke her gently, she was clutching it tightly around her body like the ultimate security blanket.

'Do you have somewhere to go?' Isobel asked, handing Alex another cup of tea and a healthy-looking muffin.

Alex shook her head.

'Would you know of someplace?' she asked, and heard her voice crack as the reality of the situation nearly overwhelmed her again.

'Well, I've one idea,' Isobel told her. 'Do you like kids?'

'Love them,' Alex replied, and to her surprise she even found a smile. 'I've done a lot of babysitting. I started when I was fourteen because I've been saving money to get a car—a red car! And I volunteer at a pre-school play group at the community centre on Saturday mornings.'

'I thought you looked familiar!' said Isobel. 'I sometimes take my twins to that play group.' She thought for a moment. 'I know this sounds daft and it's a bit sudden, but would you like to come home with me? I've got two monsters so I can promise they'll take your mind off your troubles for a while. I'll be in the house but I'll need to sleep at some time, so if you're there I can. My husband's also a doctor and he's due at work any minute and one of the twins has a cold so they can't go to kindy. Dave, that's my husband, and I have been talking about getting an au pair for some time, but neither of us has ever had time to do anything about it. You need a home—and ours might not be it—but just for today at least, would you like a job?'

This time it was Alex who hugged her!

CHAPTER ONE

SHE'D COME HOME to Heritage Port with plenty of mis-
givings, but within hours of her arrival Alex had known
she'd done the right thing. Although her childhood had
been happy, her best memories of the place were of the
three and a half years she'd spent with the Armitage family, minding the rambunctious twins, finishing school
and even starting her pre-med studies at university, she
and the twins' parents juggling their timetables so everything ran smoothly.

Well, as smoothly as could be expected with two little
mischief-makers in the house!

It wasn't that the horror of the rape and the humiliation of the trial that had followed it didn't occasionally
still disturb her dreams—her ex-fiancé had blamed it for
what he'd termed her inability to respond to his kisses,
let alone anything more intimate—but she found herself
pleased to be home in one of the most beautiful places
in the world.

As the taxi carried her from the airport, bright sun
shone on the rolling ocean, white-fringed waves crashed
on the rocks at the headland, and shushed up the beach.
The river was as green and peaceful as she remembered
it, and, best of all, somehow, in the intervening years,
the hard knot in her heart had loosened.

Now, sitting beside the hospital bed, she was able to look at her father and remember the man who'd first taught her to bait her fishing hook—the father she'd loved…

'So, where have you come from?' one of the nurses in the ICU asked as Alex, her luggage stacked in a corner of the room, held her father's hand, and talked to the sleeping man about fishing in the dark shadows of the mangroves that arched over the little inlets off the river.

'Here,' she told him. 'I've just been away for a while.'

Away when the girls she'd been at school with had been marrying and having babies…

Away when her mother had died without forgiving her for 'making a fuss'…

Away, but always waiting for a letter that said two simple words, 'Come home.'

'How long's a while?' the nurse asked, making conversation, Alex knew, but welcoming it in the sterile room, the silence broken only by her voice and the machines.

'Sixteen years.'

'Long time!'

And it had been.

When the Armitage family, with their darling twins, had shifted to Melbourne so Isobel and Dave could continue specialist careers, Alex had chosen to go north to Brisbane to finish her medical training.

From there, on Isobel's advice, she'd contacted her parents, writing to them to tell them where she was and what she was doing. Although she'd received no response, she'd continued writing—birthdays and Christmas—always somehow hoping…

Then, three weeks ago, in far-off Glasgow, she'd received a letter from her father. Her mother was dead, Rusty, the dog, was dead, Mr Spencer had died, and he, her father, was going into hospital for open-heart surgery to replace a wonky valve.

The letter hadn't asked her to come home, but here she was, sitting in the intensive care unit in the new modern hospital at Heritage Port, talking quietly to her heavily sedated father, and remembering happy times.

Will Kent, head intensivist, doing a round of the ICU, was surprised to see the woman there, her arms cradling her head on the bottom of the bed, apparently deeply asleep. Mr Hudson might be his patient in this unit, Will's fiefdom, but the man had been unconscious since he'd arrived.

'Who's the woman in with Mr Hudson?' he asked one of the nurses.

'His daughter—Alexandra, I think she's called—just arrived from Scotland. Apparently hasn't been home for years. Some daughter!'

Alexandra Hudson—Alex!

Of course she hadn't been home for years—banished as she'd been at sixteen. Ending up with his next-door neighbours, Isobel and Dave Armitage, as a nanny for their twins.

He peered more closely at the patient.

There didn't seem to be anything familiar about the man—old now, and grey with illness—but he *did* remember the day Isobel had asked him to accompany her and Alex back to the Hudson home so Alex could get some clothes. Dave had been working, and Will had felt enormously proud that Isobel had chosen him to go along. He'd seen himself as the protector of the two women—a tall, lanky, bespectacled, twenty-two-year-old protector!

Mrs Hudson had thrown Alex's clothes from an upstairs window, ranting all the time about 'whores' and 'sluts', while Mr Hudson had barred the door, standing there like an ancient biblical prophet, his only prophecy doom.

Poor Alex had been scarlet with humiliation and hurt, tears leaking from behind the big dark glasses she'd worn even inside in those days. He'd wanted to put his arm around her—to give her a hug—but he'd known she'd shy away, as she had from all but the twins' hugs and kisses.

Not that he'd have kissed her—she'd been, what? Fifteen? Sixteen?

He couldn't remember—remembered only the deep pity he'd felt for the so obviously damaged teenager.

Was this patient, here in the ICU, recovering from an operation for a heart valve replacement, *that* Mr Hudson?

Was the sleeping woman really Alex?

And had his thoughts disturbed her that she stirred and lifted her head?

Huge blue eyes she'd hidden behind darkened glasses for all the years she'd lived next door stared unseeingly at him.

Huge blue eyes framed by golden blonde hair tipped with silver here and there and softly tousled by sleep. The early beauty she'd tried to hide with shorn hair and the glasses had come to fruition. Even sleep-tousled, she was stunning.

'Alex?'

She straightened up from the bed and frowned at him.

'I'm Will, Will Kent—from next door to the Armitages, remember?'

The frown deepened and she shook her head, so obviously puzzled he had to smile.

'You pinched my job,' he added, remembering how he'd pretended to complain about losing the occasional babysitting he'd done for the Armitages.

'Superman?' she whispered, disbelief filling the words.

He flourished a pretend cloak and bowed low.

'At your service, ma'am! But also head intensivist at the hospital. Your father's in my care until he's well enough to be transferred to the coronary care unit.'

He saw her face light up as things fell into place and she shot to her feet and advanced to give him an all-enveloping hug.

'Oh, Will,' she murmured, 'it's so good to see a familiar face.'

She eased back, looking at him, then laughed.

'Not so familiar—you've grown up!'

'Not even Superman can stay twenty-two for ever,' Will said gloomily, and she laughed again, her face lighting up with delight—so gloriously beautiful Will felt his lungs seize.

Breathe, he told himself, and tried to remember how.

Fortunately, as his brain seemed to be similarly paralysed, instinct took over and his lungs filled with air while he tried to catch up with Alex's conversation.

'Intensivist? Weren't you heading towards O and G when you left Port? What made you change your mind? It can't have been the late night callouts, you'd get more of them in this job.'

'Whoa!'

Will held up his hand, pleased to see his limb was obeying messages, although other parts of his body were obviously still in shock.

'I'm on a ward round and really need to check your dad and the other patients.'

'Can we catch up later?' Alex asked. 'I couldn't get home before the op, but I've spoken to the surgeon who did the operation. He gave me the impression he wasn't too positive about the outcome.'

As Will was still feeling startling and unfamiliar re-actions to Alex's hug, he wondered if this was wise, but she was entitled to ask questions about her father's health.

But beyond that, he was intrigued. The damaged teenager who, in the beginning, would duck away if she saw him over the fence, and who'd shrunk back from any physical contact—even a simple handshake—had emerged, like a caterpillar from a cocoon, as this beau-tiful butterfly.

He wanted to know just how she'd managed the trans-formation—*and* how deep it went. He knew Isobel in par-ticular had worked hard to restore Alex's self-esteem, but there'd been a fragility about the teenager that couldn't be hidden behind dark glasses and a dreadful haircut.

'As far as your father's concerned, the operation went well, but he wasn't in the best of health before it. Other heart problems apparently. I only know this stuff from his chart but I gather that if it hadn't been a necessity...'

He paused, wondering how to tell this woman he knew but didn't know just how precarious her father's health was.

'Look, I should be through by eight and your father will still be sleeping off the anaesthetic until morning at least, so you might as well get out of here for a while,' he said. 'We *could* eat in the canteen but the food's ap-palling. There's a nice new bar and restaurant at the top of the old Royal Motel. It has a fancier name now—the motel, that is—which I can never remember. And it's in walking distance. We could have a meal—give us time to catch up.'

She nodded her agreement as a nurse came into the room. Will's attention, or ninety-five per cent of it, re-turned to his patient as he discussed Mr Hudson's progress and checked the results the monitor was revealing by the second.

Alex had slipped away, for which he was truly grateful, although he felt a momentary regret he hadn't looked at her more closely, if only to confirm his impression she'd blossomed into a startlingly beautiful woman.

Will Kent!

Alex stood in the little bathroom off the family waiting room of the ICU and smiled as she ran the name through her head.

But had the Will Kent she'd known had laughing brown eyes that crinkled with smile lines at the corners, and lips that seemed to be on the verge of a smile all the time? Of course, eighteen years ago, when he'd left Port to finish his studies, his eyes probably hadn't been crinkled, *and* they'd been hidden behind the dark-framed glasses, and, anyway, in the state she'd been in back then she wouldn't have noticed anything about any man. Certainly not his lips…

And she'd better not notice them now, she reminded herself. As she'd pointed out, Will was all grown up now, and undoubtedly married with children. In fact, throwing herself at him, hugging him, had undoubtedly embarrassed him no end, rendering him practically speechless.

Back then he'd been the Armitages' next-door neighbour christened Superman by the twins—or probably their parents, given his surname. Self-effacing—that was how she'd have described him—but somehow he'd always been around in that first year she'd been with the Armitages. In and out of the house, borrowing textbooks from Dave or Isobel, seemingly always there if she'd needed him. She tried to remember.

He'd certainly helped her rescue Riain out of the tree

one day, and had carried Rosi down to the doctor's the day she'd fallen off the swing.

Superman!

She smiled at the memories and told herself that today, with all the emotions of her return home churning inside her, she'd probably have hugged any familiar face.

An image of Will as he was now, dark hair touched with silver, lips stretched in a surprised smile, continued to linger in Alex's head, making her feel hot and embarrassed and somehow ashamed all at the same time.

Why had he suggested dinner?

He could have talked to Alex in the visitors' room, or his office, but a bar?

Had a beautiful woman giving him a hug gone straight to his head?

Or had his mother's gentle nagging—you've got to start going out again some time, Will—prompted the choice?

His mother was probably right!

He *did* have to start going out again.

Three years now—three years, eight months and five days, if he was counting—since Elise's death, and Charlotte deserved to have a mother...

He stared out at the lights sparkling in the darkened town beneath him and gave a huff of laughter.

'That would be ironic laughter,' he muttered to himself, remembering trying to explain irony to Alex, she pushing the twins on the swings while he'd leaned over the fence. Later, that was, after she'd got used to him being around and had actually asked him for some help with some assignment she was doing.

'Definitely ironic!'

'Are you talking to yourself?'

He turned to see her, and all the physical reactions he'd had at the hospital happened again.

'Never!' he lied. 'That would really label me a nut job.'

Alex smiled, intensifying all the stuff going on inside his body.

'You might think back to when I met you,' she teased. 'You were hanging upside down on the side fence, so the nut-job label was firmly in place from the beginning.'

Will gathered the tattered remnants of his dignity.

'I was being a bat!' he reminded her. 'Showing the twins how they hung in their trees.'

She laughed with such frank and open delight his insides melted.

But along with all the physical confusion came the clang of warning bells.

They were both damaged people, besides which she was probably married, or engaged, or partnered—too beautiful to still be single—while he was no catch—single father still hurting from the loss of his wife, shying away from the very thought of love. Not that this was a date…

'Are you okay?'

'I guess,' he answered the still smiling woman, although okay was a long way off.

He was sitting at a table that had a view over the mouth of the river and up along the coast as far as a distant headland.

The view provided the distraction he needed.

'Can we see your house from here?' he asked, looking not out to sea but up the river.

Alex looked too, checking the scattering of houses on the far side of the river from the town—reached by ferry during its operating hours or by a long detour back around via the highway when the ferry stopped at midnight.

'I think so,' she said. 'You see the ferry down by the wharf and the fishermen's co-op on it—the shed-looking thing? Beyond that there's the bit of waste land and the huge old fig tree—well, we're two houses down from the tree, although you probably can't see the house because they seem to have built an enormous place beside it.'

She smiled and shrugged her shoulders.

'*We're* two houses down,' she repeated. 'It's funny talking about "my house" when I haven't been there for so long. Although I didn't make it back in time to see Dad before the operation, we'd spoken on the phone a couple of times, and he'd been so upset about what had happened in the past that I promised when I came I'd stay with him, at least until he's over the op.'

Will smiled, brown eyes twinkling in his tanned face, and Alex immediately regretted this reunion.

It was because he was a familiar face that she was noticing little things about him—like the twinkling eyes.

And she certainly shouldn't be noticing twinkling eyes when he was wearing a wedding ring.

She touched his finger.

'You're married, that's nice. Kids?'

The twinkle disappeared and Will's open, friendly face went completely blank.

'Let's get you a drink first.'

He was on his feet, waiting for her order.

On his feet too quickly?

Far too quickly!

Get with it, Alex!

'G and T in a long glass, please.'

That's better. Or it would have been if she hadn't watched him walk towards the bar, seeing the breadth of his shoulders and how his back sloped down to slim hips and—

You will *not* look at his butt! The man is married, he is off limits, he's nothing more than an old—not exactly friend but someone she *had* known quite well.

It's just that he's the first familiar face you've seen that you're reacting this way.

He brought her drink and a small bowl of cashews for them to share, then settled back down at the table, this time looking out at the stretch of beach.

Do I ask again? Alex wondered, as an uneasy silence hovered around them.

'I'm a single father,' he began, still staring out along the beach. 'My wife died when Charlotte was born—cancer—Charlotte's three and a half.'

Will turned back to his companion as he spoke, aware of how stiff and remote he must have sounded as he'd blurted out his story.

Lack of practice in telling it—he knew that. Telling it was one of the reasons he'd avoided going out—telling it hurt...

Had she felt that pain—heard it in his voice—that her fingers, cold and slightly damp from the glass, reached out and took his hand, giving it a squeeze?

'Oh, Will,' she said softly. 'I cannot imagine what pain that must have caused you—and what a loss it must have been. We see awful things every day in our work, yet we somehow think we're immune to it.'

She hesitated, her fingers tightening on his hand.

'Do you want to talk about it—to tell me?'

And suddenly he did. It was almost as if he'd been waiting for Alex to return—or someone like Alex to come along—so he could put it all together and let it all out, releasing some of the terrible tension he'd carried inside his body for so long.

'We met as students, married after graduation then waited a while to have kids—an intern's life is appalling so we were hardly ever together. Then, when we decided to have a family, Elise, her name was Elise, was diagnosed with breast cancer when she was three months pregnant. It was a very aggressive strain and the specialists wanted her to abort the baby and get immediate treatment. She refused, knowing the treatment would leave her sterile.'

He paused but Alex kept quiet, perhaps sensing there was more.

'We fought about it, Alex,' he finally added, looking into the blue eyes across the table from him, seeing her understanding and concern. "That's what hurts so much now, that I fought her over this, said terrible things.'

'But only out of love,' Alex said quietly, and he knew she understood.

'She wouldn't accept any treatment or even pain relief that would have crossed the placenta and harmed the baby, and by the last month of the pregnancy she was in a coma—treatment was too late.'

Alex sipped her drink, knocked flat by the deep pain behind Will's simple tale. To her, in that first year at the Armitages', Will had always seemed like part of the family. And, perhaps because of the family link, he'd been totally unthreatening, unlike the youths and young men she'd see on the street or in the park—males who'd make some casual remark, not really even aimed at her, but enough to make her cringe and scurry back home with the twins.

Will had just been Will, studying medicine because, she suspected, he'd idolised Dave and Isobel.

Now the pain he'd had in his life made her heart ache for him.

No wonder he'd grown up…

'So, your daughter?'

His smile lit up his face.

It did weird things to her insides too, but she could ignore them.

'Charlotte,' he said simply. 'She's the greatest—a precious gift—she's why we came back here to Port. Look, here's a photo.'

Alex waited while he pulled out his wallet and dug in the folds, and she wondered if he was giving himself time to get over the memories of his wife's death.

The small, wallet-sized photo, showed a little girl with a mop of brown curls and a smile that could melt stone. Alex's breathing faltered as she looked at the beautiful child. Mr Spencer had stolen more than her innocence, he'd stolen her ability to get close enough to a man to want a sexual relationship, let alone a child.

But Will was speaking again and she switched off the futile regrets to listen.

'Mum minds her when I'm at work, although I've built a separate flat in Mum's house so we're independent a lot of the time.'

The happiness faded from his face.

'It worries me, though, that I rely so much on Mum. Now she's retired she should be out doing things, not minding a nearly four-year-old.'

'I bet she's fine with that,' Alex told him, and touched the hand that still held the photo, just gently…

'She says so and it will be easier when Charlotte goes to kindy next year, then school—'

'And then, whoosh—they're gone from your life.'

His smile wasn't the worst one she'd ever seen, but it was close, yet even the weak effort affected Alex.

Jet-lag—it had to be!

Jet-lag and seeing a familiar face, that's all that was going on.

She let go of his hand and concentrated on her drink.

'So, tell me about you,' he said, and she knew her own smile would be even weaker than his had been.

In so many ways it was a success story, yet—

'Perhaps we should eat,' she suggested, hoping a move from this table—any kind of movement—might...

What? Make him forget he'd asked?

Or break the sense of intimacy—it had to be a false intimacy because of the past—that seemed to be enclosing them.

'We can talk over food,' she added, because she knew she'd been far too abrupt.

Will stood up with such alacrity she had to believe he'd felt it too. He led her into another part of the room where most of the diners already finishing their meals, lingering over dessert or last drinks.

'Tell me about Charlotte—favourite games, toys, books,' she said, when a waiter had ushered them to a table and slid serviettes onto their laps.

Will grinned at her, which kind of undid a lot of what the move had accomplished, in that a different kind of tension had appeared, tightening her skin and skidding along her nerves.

'You're supposed to be telling me about you,' he reminded her.

Alex waved away his objection but he ignored the gesture.

'No way, you tell first,' he ordered, waggling his finger at her, like a teacher with a reluctant pupil.

'Here's the short version,' Alex said. 'You'd gone south

to finish your degree before I left the Armitages', but I got that scholarship Isobel made me work so hard for, went to Brisbane, got my degree, got engaged—church upbringing still strong, so marriage seemed a logical step. I'd wanted to specialise in cardiology, Dave's influence, I suppose, although I couldn't handle the surgery. I was offered a terrific training job in London, qualified, got unengaged, moved from London to Glasgow, and now I'm home.'

Given that Will was still smiling at her, she thought she'd done rather well.

'That's it?' he asked. 'What happened to the fiancé? And you're a beautiful woman, why only one?'

She'd been pretending to study the menu while she'd talked but now she looked directly at Will.

'I was so sure I'd recovered from the rape—been to counsellors, talked and talked,' she said, pleased to hear how calmly she could say the word, even back here where it had happened.

She paused then admitted something she'd never before put into words.

'But relationships—they just don't seem to work. Not that I've had that many, but I've tried, Will, I really have, but when it comes to taking the next step—the intimacy thing—I pull back. It's unfair to the men, apart from anything else, so in the end I stopped dating and, really, my life is simpler and I'm happy with it. There's something missing in me, Will, and that's all I can put it down to.'

Had she sounded depressed that Will reached out and covered her hand with his?

Nothing more than a sympathetic touch, but it fired Alex's slowly settling nerves again. She removed her hand to close her menu.

'I think I'll have the rack of lamb,' she said, far too brightly.

* * *

Will waved the waiter over, gave their order, talked to him about a good red wine to have with the lamb. They would sell it by the glass, which was all he wanted.

The waiter returned with a bottle of red, showed it to Will, offered him a taste, then poured them both a glass.

Will lifted his to toast Alex, who clinked her glass with his and kind of smiled. Maybe it would have worked if sadness hadn't still been lingering in her eyes...

Not that he'd meant to notice her eyes—

'So, Glasgow? What on earth were you doing there?'

This time Alex's smile was better, and he heard an echo of laughter in her voice.

'It's actually a very lively city, and I had a dream job. Then Dad got in touch and—well, here I am. As I said, I'm a cardiologist and although I hope I won't get a lot of intensive-care patients, I imagine we'll see a bit of each other around the hospital. I've joined a practice here.'

'Brian Lane's?'

Alex nodded.

'But that's great, he's a good friend of mine,' Will said, smiling enthusiastically. 'I have a room in the same building—we'll be running into each other all the time.'

Before Alex could reply—well, what *was* there to reply—the smile faded from Will's face and he asked, rather uncertainly, 'It *is* good, isn't it?'

His sudden uncertainty told Alex that he was as un-practised in the relationship game as she was. Not that this was a relationship. Will was still obviously getting over Elise, while she, Alex, could make an epic disaster of even a casual date.

'I think it's good,' she said quietly. 'You've already made my homecoming so much easier, Will, so having

you around as I learn my way around the hospital will
be fantastic.'

His face lit up as his luminous smile returned, and
Alex was swamped by a shivery sensation of…

What?

Happiness?

No, that would be ridiculous.

Fortunately, the waiter returned with their dinners,
and operating on her rack of lamb, separating out the cutlets, gave Alex time to recover from whatever it might
have been.

Will was talking about Charlotte now, apparently
answering the questions Alex had asked earlier in the
conversation.

And in every word Alex heard the love this grown-up
Will had for his little daughter, while the happiness she'd
brought him shone in his eyes.

'She sounds great,' Alex said, and to her surprise Will
blushed, much as he had as a young man when she'd
caught him hanging on the fence.

'I talk too much about her when I do go out. Mum
says I need to do some speed dating to get back into the
way of speaking to women. She says Charlotte needs a
mother and she's probably right.'

Serious brown eyes met Alex's across the table.

'But I've got out of the dating habit,' he admitted, before adding ruefully, 'Not that I was ever that good at
it. Do you remember Isobel telling me—some time that
year—that I should write out a list of things to talk about
before going to a party? Questions, she said, ask women
questions about themselves and actually listen to their
answers—that's very flattering.'

Alex smiled.

'I suspected at the time she was talking to me as well.

She kept encouraging me to go out and meet young people. As I remember, you were all of a dither because you thought this girl you liked would be there, right?'

She studied Will, whose entire attention now appeared to be on his meal.

'Did it work for you?' she asked.

He looked up and smiled, and although the now-familiar reactions to his smile tumbled through her body, they stilled when he answered.

'It did,' he said quietly. 'The girl was Elise.'

Which killed that conversation dead, Will realised as the words landed between them with an almost audible thump.

He had to think, to say something—anything—because talking to Alex was making him feel good inside, while looking at Alex—well, best he didn't consider how *that* was making him feel!

But where was his list?

Ask questions, Isobel had told him way back then.

He stopped pretending to be eating and looked up at the woman across the table from him, delicately cutting morsels of lamb from her cutlets.

'How did you feel about coming back to Port?'

She met his eyes, and smiled.

'Ask questions, huh?' she teased, then looked thoughtful, as if actually considering her reply.

'Hearing from my father—that was a shock. After so many years, it took a while to take it in, but then I reread his letter, saw the bit about his health, and coming back seemed the only possible thing to do—the natural thing. As if it was time...'

How could he not reach out to rest his hand on hers?

How could he not squeeze her slim, warm fingers?

'It must be hard,' he said, and her smile brightened.

'I don't really know yet,' she said. 'In the taxi, coming from the airport, seeing the river and the sea, well, it *felt* right. In fact, I felt a surge of excitement, as if this was where I should be. But since then I've been at the hospital and then here—not really home at all.'

'But you'll go home—to your old house—stay there?'

She nodded.

'I think so—for a while at least, while Dad convalesces, then we'll see how it works out. It's been nearly twenty years since I left home, Will, and I don't really know him any more.'

Her smile this time was less joyous, nothing more than a slight curl of her lips, and her eyes held Will's as she added, 'It might sound strange but up to that time I was happy here, you see. I had a wonderful childhood with the river right beside us. I think I've let what happened to me affect my life for far too long. I want to start again, back in the place where I belong.'

He wanted to kiss her, in praise of her courage, nothing more—well, almost nothing more.

'If anyone can do it, you can,' he said.

'Thanks,' she said softly, lifting her hand from under his and replacing it on top, where it sat, warm and comforting, although wasn't he supposed to be comforting her?

She really should stop holding his hand. This was just a dinner between colleagues—old friends—not a date.

But holding Will's hand felt...*nice.* Pathetic word but it covered the situation.

Very nice would be even better—

A low ping of a message arriving on Will's mobile broke into her thoughts, and the gravity on his face as he read the message told her it wasn't good news.

'I'm sorry, Alex, but your father's had a setback—

heart attack or stroke. His surgeon is on his way, but I'll have to go.'

'I'll come with you,' Alex said.

Will was on his feet, asking the waiter to put the dinner on his account, shrugging into the jacket he'd hung on the back of his chair.

'I'm so sorry,' he said to Alex as he walked her to the door, slipping a comforting arm around her shoulders and giving her a hug. 'His surgeon was worried about him undergoing the operation when he'd had a heart attack three years ago but the leaking heart valve was restricting his life and eventually would have killed him. Now this!'

Will insisted on driving her to the hospital.

'I can drop you back at your car later,' he said.

'No car. I got a cab from the airport earlier and walked from the hospital this evening,' Alex whispered, while all the 'what ifs' clamoured in her head. She should have come sooner, tried harder to heal the wound between herself and her parents, at the very least thanked Dad for getting in touch with her in the end.

Now it might be too late. A post-surgical patient was too fragile to have heroic lifesaving measures practised on him.

'He'd signed a health directive stating he didn't want to be resuscitated,' Will said quietly as he opened the door of his car for her.

Alex found a wan smile.

'I was just thinking he was hardly a candidate for the more heroic revival techniques.'

Will patted her hand. 'Let's wait and see.' He closed the car door and walked around the hood to get in beside her.

They arrived at the ICU to find a flurry of activity as they prepared to take the patient to Radiography for a CT scan of his brain, a stroke now seeming the most likely cause of his deep unconsciousness.

Alex stood beside her father's bed, with Will on the other side.

'If it's a stroke it would have to be haemorrhagic, rather than a clot—he'd be on blood thinners post-op,' Alex said, trying to think professionally so she could block out the emotion and nerves.

Will nodded glumly. 'Any bleed with already thinned blood could be catastrophic.'

Alex watched helplessly as gentle hands stripped away the tubes and monitors before lifting her father onto the scanner's stretcher and sliding his head into the machine.

In ten minutes they had the answer, a subarachnoid haemorrhage where an unsuspected aneurysm had burst.

Her father was returned to his bed and reattached to monitors and breathing apparatus, but Alex knew it was too late. Such a catastrophic bleed had only one outcome, especially in her father's weakened post-op state.

And heroics, had any been available, weren't an option. Within an hour of them returning to the hospital her father was dead. Alex looked down at the man who, in her childhood, had been so good to her. It had been a strict upbringing, but Dad had been patient, and caring, and always kind.

Until the end…

She looked across the bed at Will, who'd stayed quietly there to support her.

'I suppose I'll have to organise a funeral in that damn church!' she muttered, again using practicalities to keep the fear and pain at bay. 'And face those women who spat at me when I took their precious Mr Spencer to court.'

'I don't think so,' Will said, something in his voice making her look up from the figure on the bed. 'I get to see the health directives of all patients coming into the ICU, and also any personal requests in the event of a patient's death. Your father left very specific instructions. There were to be no services at all, from memory.'

'Poor Dad,' Alex whispered, then she turned away from the bed, aware that tears were close to falling and not wanting to give in to the mix of rage and grief inside her until she was on her own. 'I'd better get home and go through his papers and just hope he left some instructions.'

Will could hear the tears thick in her voice, and knew instinctively she wouldn't want to cry in front of him. The teenager who'd lived next door was all grown up now, and he had to respect her adulthood for all he wanted to take her in his arms and comfort her.

He insisted on driving her home, aware that if he missed the last ferry he'd have a long drive out to the highway and back into town, but he knew she'd been tired and jet-lagged before her father's death had hit her, and he didn't want her returning to that house of hurt on her own.

He kept the headlights shining on the front of the house, while she dug around under pot plants for a spare key.

'It's always here,' she muttered when he joined the search, and it was he who found the hollow rock among the pebbles on the path.

He unlocked the door for her and pushed it open, wondering just how hard this would be for her. She was standing back, just a little, and he sensed she was gathering the nerve to walk into the place that had once been her home.

He was about to suggest she stay somewhere else—at his mother's place or a hotel in town—just for tonight when an unnerving voice yelled from the darkness.

'That you, Bruce?'

To Will's surprise, Alex laughed and laughed, stepping past him and reaching out to switch on a light, calling, 'Buddy, where are you? It's Alex, Buddy.'

The pink and grey galah shot like an arrow down the hall, landing on Alex's head and dancing a little jig there before settling on her shoulder, turning his head a little to one side as he studied her, then letting loose with a loud 'Who's a pretty girl, then?' as he nuzzled his head against her cheek.

Now the tears she'd held in check spilled from her eyes, although through the dampness she was smiling.

'Silly bird,' she said, turning back to Will. 'We've had him since he was a fledgling and we have no idea where he got the name Bruce, but no amount of patience on Dad's part ever got him to say another name. He talks a lot of other rot, but he always comes back to Bruce.'

The galah was brushing his feathers against the tears as if to dry them up, and seeing the love between the pair made Will's heart twist, but at least the bird had made it easier for Alex to step back into her childhood home.

She had found a tissue and finished the mopping up operations.

'Thanks, Will, for everything,' she said quietly. 'Not only for now but for before, because that first year with the Armitages you were always around and so—so *normal* you helped me be normal too. I'll be okay now I'm home—home with Buddy. I've left my luggage in the visitors' room of the CCU, but I can collect it tomorrow. I imagine there'll be a ton of forms to fill out and arrangements to be made.'

He was being dismissed in the nicest possible way and although he'd have liked to help her—to save her the pain of making arrangements for her father whatever they might be—he knew he had to go.

He touched her shoulder and, daring the bird to object, kissed her lightly on the cheek.

'You thought he'd take your eyes out, didn't you?' Alex teased, smiling now, then she reached out and gave him a hug. 'Thanks again!'

He walked away, aware of the woman in the lighted doorway, blue eyes watching his departure, a pink and grey bird dancing on her shoulder, still enquiring about the whereabouts of Bruce.

CHAPTER TWO

THE RAUCOUS CRIES of 'Where's Bruce?' woke Alex long before she'd have liked to awaken, but as the bird was sitting on the pillow beside her head and tugging at her hair, she gave in and clambered out of bed.

Blearily making her way to the kitchen, surprised by how automatic her movements through the house were, she made a coffee and took it out onto the big deck that looked over the river, suddenly glad to be awake as the rising sun turned the placid waters pink and mauve and gold in turn. She breathed deeply, taking in the eucalypt-scented air, watching an osprey swirl across the sky in search of breakfast, hearing the putt-putt of dinghy engines as fisherman set out up the river to set their crab pots or try their luck with lines.

Another breath…

Yes, she was home.

All the pain of long ago hadn't damaged the sense that this was where she belonged—maybe not for ever, or even for very long—heaven knew what the future held—but for now it was enough.

Not quite enough to heal the pain of the past or the loss of the man she'd come home to make peace with—only time would do that—but here she could handle it, cope with it, do whatever had to be done.

Finishing her coffee, she walked back into the kitchen, surprised to find a note she hadn't noticed earlier, although it was propped in a prominent spot on the sill of the window looking out over the deck.

Thank you for coming, Alexandra. I hope with all my heart you will stay here at the house. Bacon and eggs in fridge, fruit and veg in the bottom drawers, and meat in the freezer.

Later we'll talk but for now it is enough to know that you are here.

Please forgive me.

Love, Dad.

Alex smoothed the paper, willing away the tears, then held it to her cheek as if she could feel her father's touch in it.

A noise out the front—on the road side of the house—turned her in that direction. Buddy was still on the veranda railing, giving cheek to the gulls and oystercatchers on the mudflats of the river.

The noise was barely there—someone trying to be quiet—but surely not a burglar at this time of the morning.

She made her way to the front room and peered through the curtains. A dark maroon SUV was parked outside, the driver's side door open. Had Will's car been maroon?

But why would he be sneaking around outside her house at the crack of dawn?

One way to find out. She walked down the hall and opened the door, and there he was, as large as life.

'You shouldn't open a door like that—you should have a locked screen or a spyhole in the door.'

Alex laughed, and hoped it was because of his lecturing tone, not because she was glad to see him.

'I brought your luggage from the hospital and the forms you'll need to fill in. Apparently your father had left instructions for his body to go to the university. It was with his health directive and a note from the university telling you whom to contact. I was going to leave the papers with the baggage—I thought you'd still be sleeping.'

'When I've got a bird who's better than any alarm clock?' Alex complained, as Buddy swooped back from the deck to inspect the visitor.

'He's obviously disappointed I'm not Bruce,' Will said, holding out his hand towards the bird, who eyed him cautiously for a moment before condescending to jump onto Will's forearm.

Alex watched the little scene, curiously unsettled by it, not just Buddy on Will's arm, but Will being here at all. But she could hardly leave him standing on the doorstep with her luggage.

Yet asking him in seemed...not dangerous—it couldn't possibly be dangerous as this was Will...

'He must be missing Dad,' she said, mainly to avoid a decision. Buddy had walked up Will's arm and was perched on his shoulder, nibbling gently at his earlobe. 'He's usually very shy with strangers.'

Two o'clock in the morning—that's when Will had reached the decision to collect Alex's luggage from the hospital and see what he could do as far as the paperwork was concerned. If he went early, he'd decided, she would probably still be asleep and he could leave the lot in the front porch.

That way he'd avoid seeing Alex, and as images of her and replays of their evening had already kept him awake for hours, he'd come to the realisation that the less he saw of her the better.

At least until he'd sorted out a few things in his mind and body. His body's reaction to her was understandable enough, she was a beautiful woman, but the voice in his head that kept whispering 'hurt' and 'vulnerable' and other warning words was a different matter.

He'd already worked out, at least a year ago, that when he did find a mother for Charlotte, it would be a different kind of marriage. Two mature people finding companionship and sexual satisfaction and, yes, love of a kind, but not *love* love.

Love love hurt too much when you lost it—devastated and destroyed you. There was no way he could go through that again—and Alex, with the pain of her past, deserved better than some lukewarm version of the real thing.

So now he was standing at her front door, a galah on his head, feeling like an absolute galoot.

'Thank you so much,' Alex said, and he felt a stab of disappointment, sure he was about to be dismissed. Not that he'd expected to be invited in—hadn't expected her to be up—but, seeing her in too-small, pink, floral pyjamas, he really didn't want to go.

'Have you had breakfast?' she asked.

Hope rose again.

'No, Charlotte's stayed over with Mum because I'm on call this weekend so I thought I'd drop this stuff off early so you'd have it when you woke up. Thought it would save you dashing over to the hospital to get some clothes to wear.'

She smiled and the day seemed brighter, and while his head might be calling him all kinds of a fool, his heart swelled just a little in his chest and beat a little faster.

Attraction, that's all it was—physical attraction after too long a celibacy. But knowing that didn't stop him carrying her suitcases inside, the bird now flying in front of him as if to show him the way.

Alex led the way up to her bedroom, then, aware of how girlish it still looked—her bedroom at sixteen— she hesitated.

'Just leave them here in the hall, I'll sort them out from there. Dad left a note about food in the fridge and I was about to cook a hearty breakfast before facing whatever lay ahead.'

She turned towards him.

'Now it seems you've handled most of what lay immediately ahead, so the least I can do is feed you.'

She looked worried, puzzled, uncertain—exactly the way Will felt—but she recovered first, offering a rueful smile as she said, 'It's weird, isn't it, meeting again like this?'

Weird didn't begin to sum it up! Although why, he couldn't fathom...

'Go and sit on the deck,' she told him when they reached the kitchen, and he saw the majestic sweep of the river through the windows. 'Bacon and eggs okay? And I've coffee made if you'd like a cup while you wait.'

To Alex's relief, Will accepted a cup of coffee and headed out onto the deck, lessening, though not by much, the tension in her nerves. She was reasonably certain the attraction she was feeling towards him was nothing more than his familiarity. Coming home had been like landing in another life, and he was a familiar figure to cling to while she found her way around.

Not that she could cling to Will.

It had been more than three years since his wife had died and even though he'd said he'd got out of the dating

habit, there had to have been other women in his life—
or another special woman.

And, anyway, it felt wrong, this attraction to him. If
he was looking for a woman he'd be thinking in terms of
a mother for Charlotte—someone stable and committed
to both him and his daughter.

And given the mess she'd made of relationships in the
past, she'd hardly qualify for either role.

The bacon was sizzling and she pushed it to one side
of the pan and added eggs.

'How do you like your eggs?' she called through the
window.

'Sunny side up,' he replied, and the fact that she liked
hers that way as well did not mean one damn thing!

She made toast, set it, butter, salt and pepper, honey
and marmalade on a tray with their cutlery and carried
the lot out to the table, then hurried back in for the plates
before Will could offer to help her.

Distance, that's all she needed. A bit of distance between them and all the unwanted and inexplicable physical reactions in her body would eventually disappear.

Will watched the river come to life, fishing boats mo-
toring towards the mouth, kayakers paddling furiously
past, one lone windsurfer trying desperately to stay upright in the lightest of breezes.

He'd have breakfast then leave and, really, was there
any reason he'd have to see Alex again?

No reason at all, and it was definitely best that he
didn't—

Though why?

He tried to work out why the instant attraction he'd
felt towards her seemed so wrong. Almost dangerous.

How could it be?

Because instant attraction didn't work?

Because she'd admitted being bad at relationships and he didn't want to upset Charlotte by bringing a woman who might not stick with them into her life?

Or because such a strong attraction could lead to love?

Wasn't that the crux of it?

Seventeen years ago she'd been, to him, the kid who'd shifted in next door. A kid in all kinds of pain—that had been obvious.

He realised, as the word 'kid' came into his thoughts again, that that was how he'd always seen her. The kid who'd minded the twins, a quiet shadow in the house next door.

Although he'd realised just how much inner strength she'd had when her rape case had come to court, one long year after the complaint. The Armitages—either Dave or Isobel—had always gone with her when she'd had to appear right up until the day of the judgment. Dave had been down south at a conference and Isobel had asked Will to accompany her and Alex, somehow guessing the verdict wasn't going to be the one they wanted.

He'd been there on one side of her, Isobel on the other, and her hand had gripped his as the jury pronounced the rapist not guilty.

He'd been so proud to have known her as she'd stood up, head high, fixed Mr Spencer with a withering look and marched out of the court.

'At least,' she'd said to her two supporters, 'other people will be suspicious of him now and he'll be too scared to touch another child.'

He glanced up as the woman who'd been the 'kid next door' slid a tray onto the table. 'I'd forgotten just how wonderful it was to sit out here.'

'It's fantastic,' he agreed, taking in the too-small floral

pyjamas again and wondering if it was possible to keep thinking of her in that 'kid next door' way.

She passed him his plate, refilled his coffee cup, and settled beside him so they could both look out at the river.

No, came the answer to his wondering. If anything, the pyjamas accentuated her womanliness, somehow emphasising the softness of the body inside them, straining buttons suggesting how much she'd filled out.

'I think I've figured out that it's Saturday,' she said, pausing in her obvious enjoyment of breakfast. 'Does that mean you have the day off?'

Ordinary question—work question really. Talking of work would be good. But before he could reply she was talking again.

'I was only asking, and I know it's a cheek when you've done so much already, bringing my stuff and Dad's papers from the hospital, but if you don't have to rush off, and don't have anything planned with your daughter, I wondered…'

Her voice trailed off and, instead of watching the river, she was studying her bacon and eggs as if they were some rare anatomical discovery.

'I'm on call, which means Charlotte is with Mum. I don't have to rush off unless I'm paged,' he said. 'So out with it.'

She looked up, her face turned to his, serious, worried, a shade embarrassed.

'I know I've been in the house since late last night, but really only in my old bedroom and the kitchen and I kind of went to both of those automatically, if you know what I mean. It's not that I'm scared—but—'

An abrupt break this time, but he thought he'd caught on. He shooed Buddy away before the bird stole a second piece of bacon, and touched Alex lightly on the shoulder.

'You want me to go through the house with you, just be there while you do it the first time?'

She nodded, her embarrassment obvious now as colour rose in her cheeks.

'I know it's stupid,' she said, straightening in her chair and taking a deep breath, 'but it's been so long, nearly twenty years, and walking into their bedroom, the living room, downstairs into Dad's workshop—'

'Will be traumatic enough even with company,' Will finished for her.

She smiled her agreement, just a wan little smile, but Will's body responded to it as automatically as she'd gone to her bedroom the previous night. He leaned forward and kissed her, just a quick gentle kiss, on lips that tasted of bacon and coffee and something indefinable, which he had to assume was just Alex.

'It'll be okay,' he assured her. 'Everything will work out.'

Heaven help me, Alex thought. She was having enough trouble coping with her return to this house, her father's death and Will's presence, without him kissing her. Not that it had been a kiss kiss, just a comfort kiss, but her body hadn't seemed to recognise the difference and her nerves were twittering with excitement.

And she'd asked him to walk through the house with her, so he wasn't leaving any time soon!

He was focussed on his breakfast—or possibly on keeping Buddy from eating it—so she could sneak a look at him. Maybe if she looked enough, she could work out why he was affecting her the way he was.

Lovely profile—maybe not such a good idea, the looking—straight nose, just enough chin, and a forehead that was broad and smooth, the dark hair just a little long so a bit flopped across it in a rather endearing way.

Endearing way? Are you out of your mind, woman?

But her looking had fixed on the lips that had just kissed her—well, touched hers in a sympathetic-friend kind of way.

They were pale, and delineated by an even paler line around them, not that they needed the delineation because they were very nicely made, not too full or fleshy but not mean and straight. Without doubt, the man had great lips.

Which, of course, led to her wayward mind wondering what a real kiss from those lips would feel like.

'Gone to sleep sitting up?' Will asked, fortunately *after* she'd taken her eyes off his lips and was gazing sightlessly out over the river.

'Just about,' she answered, smiling at him to show how awake she was and how unaffected she'd been by his presence, and the kiss, and her perusal of his profile.

Liar!

'So, we'll be off on our expedition?' he asked, and she forgot her confusion over Will as all the anxiety about really seeing the house—her home?—returned.

'Best we do,' she managed, stacking their plates on the tray and standing up to take it back to the kitchen.

'Let me,' he said, his eyes meeting hers, his fingers brushing lightly against her hands as he removed the tray from her weakening grasp.

With the dirty dishes deposited safely in the kitchen, Alex led the way first to the living room.

'I don't know why I've felt so—so reluctant to do this,' she said, aware she was standing far too close to Will but too disturbed by the past for it to bother her body.

Much!

'Too much pain in the past,' Will said, putting his arm around her shoulders and drawing her even closer. 'No matter how convinced we are that we've got over it, any trauma in childhood or adolescence must leave an emotional...' He hesitated, then said, 'I suppose "bruise" is as good a word as any. It's there but you don't realise it still hurts until you touch it.'

'You're right,' she agreed, leaving the comfort of that arm and stepping into the room, looking around at the bare mantelpiece above the fireplace where once pictures of her, from babyhood to teenage years, had been arrayed. Now a forlorn vase of plastic—or maybe silk—irises made an attempt to brighten up the room.

And failed dismally.

The furniture was new, which was good, but the little nest of tables that had been her grandmother's was still tucked to one side of the three-seater, and her mother's magazine stand was beside the chair in the place that had always been designated as her father's—fishing magazines in place of the gossip magazines her mother, for all her religious beliefs, had loved.

Wandering around the room, she touched the mantelpiece, the old brass screen that stood in front of the fireplace, the little nest of tables.

'Ghosts?' Will asked, and she was surprised by her reply.

'No, not at all! It's different, but that's about it. And it's still a comfortable room. I think fireplaces do that, don't you?'

Before he could reply she was leading the way upstairs. Bathrooms were bathrooms and the downstairs one held no memories—bad or good—but her parents' bedroom—who knew?

But when she walked into it she stopped, looking all around, unable to believe her mother's once frilly, pale blue and green bedroom had been transformed into what looked more like a monastic cell than a frequently slept-in space.

Gone was the big bed that had dominated the room, replaced by a large single pressed up against a wall, made up with military precision, not a wrinkle to be seen. Next to it her father had set one of the pair of old bedside tables, and on it he'd had a lamp, a picture of his bride and himself on their wedding day, and as many of the photos off the mantelpiece as he could fit. Photos of Alex from babyhood to her last school photo, the plain navy uniform of the church-based school, also wrinkle-free—obviously in honour of the photo day.

'I can't believe it,' she whispered, touching the photos then turning to cross the room to the cupboards built into one wall. Her father's suits were neatly hung in about a tenth of the wardrobe space, while his shorts and polo shirts, his underwear and socks were all set out on the shelves, aligned to meet and pass any inspection.

'It's as if he tried to get rid of all traces of her,' she murmured, more to herself than to Will. 'Do you suppose he did it when she died, or when he knew I was coming home?'

It wasn't a question anyone could answer, so Will didn't try, but he was concerned by how the changes in the room had affected Alex, and couldn't help but wonder just how much of the past might come back to haunt her in this place that had been her home.

'Are you sure you're okay, living here, even for a while?' he asked, as she turned in the centre of the room, taking in the bareness yet again. His heart ached to help her, but who could help someone suffer pain?

'Mum's got a spare bedroom if you'd like to camp there until you make a decision about where you'd like to live,' he heard himself say, though common sense had been relentless in telling him the less he saw of Alex the better.

After all, what could he offer her, still grieving himself over the loss of Elise?

To his relief—at least, he thought it was relief—she smiled and shook her head.

'Leave my river view? I might have been away from it for a long time, but it's always been there in my head, and no matter how unhappy my leaving here was, nothing could take away the pleasure I will get from just being by the river—*my* river!'

The smile brightened, and she added, 'Do you really not have to go to work?'

'As long as I'm not paged and I pop in to show my face later today, I'm covered,' he said, and her smile grew mischievous.

'Then let's go down and see if Dad's tinnie is still under the house. Knowing him, the boat should be in top condition. We can go out on the river and down some of the offshoots where I used to take the twins fishing.' She paused before adding, 'Didn't you come with us once because Isobel was worried I couldn't handle the twins in the boat on my own?'

Her vague memory of the outing confirmed what Will already knew—that he'd played a very insignificant part of her life with the family next door.

She was already heading down the stairs, and he followed, out the front door and around to the river side of the house, where the slope of the ground meant there was plenty of room under the wide deck for a workshop and an aluminium dinghy on a small trailer. The ubiquitous Aussie tinnie!

Slightly bemused, he watched as Alex lifted a petrol container and placed it in the boat, close to the outboard

engine, then hooked up the fuel line, pumped it a couple
of times, and pulled the rope start on the engine.

It roared to life and, satisfied, she turned it off, and
walked to the prow to pull the trailer down to the water.

'Are you going like that?' Will asked, and she looked
down at herself in surprise.

'Good grief, you might have told me I was still in my
pyjamas, and very old pyjamas at that! What if you take
off your shoes and get the boat into the water while I
duck upstairs and change?'

She'd walked away but spun back to add, 'Probably
into something as old and ill-fitting as these pyjamas. I
doubt any of my Glasgow clothes will cope with going
out in the tinnie, but as all my old clothes—well, the ones
Mum didn't throw at me that day—are still in my bedroom, I'm sure I'll be able to find something.'

She reappeared in shorts, her long legs pale from a
Scottish winter, and a T-shirt that definitely was a little
too small.

Not that he should be noticing the way her breasts
pushed against it!

He was ordered into the middle seat, and those long,
pale legs pushed the little boat out into deeper water, Alex
swinging into it as soon as they were far enough out to
lower the motor, then they were chugging away, the light
breeze from their movement pushing her hair back from
her face as she lifted it to the sun and smiled with what
looked like sheer joy.

'How could I have stayed away from this for so long?'
she asked, expertly avoiding a youth on a jet ski and taking them closer to shore, to where a gap suddenly appeared in the mangroves.

She moved the tiller gently and they eased into a deep

green cave, sunlight filtering through the mangrove branches meeting over their heads.

'It's like another world,' she whispered, and he had to agree. Beneath the boat the water was dark green and very mysterious, while the weird shapes and tangles of mangrove roots suggested hiding places or homes for elves and fairies.

'Dad bought me a little tinnie when I was five. It had a very simple motor, only one half horsepower so I could use it without a licence, and this was my very favourite place.'

Will felt a now familiar squelch of his heart. How was it that this particular woman could touch him as she did? It wasn't part of the attraction business, strong though that was. It was different, strange but wonderful at the same time.

He gave up on the puzzle and simply enjoyed the beauty and the solitude, the quiet broken only by the humming of bees and the twitter of an occasional bird...

CHAPTER THREE

'Best we get back,' Alex said, when they'd drifted across the shadowy water to the end of the inlet. She glanced over at him. 'I've been meaning to ask, why Intensive Care?'

Will turned from his fascination with the mangroves and smiled at her. 'Too stupid to decide which specialty?'

'I doubt that very much,' Alex replied, although she wondered if it had been a stupid question. His wife had been in a coma—he'd have spent a lot of time in Intensive Care...

Hoping to cover her insensitivity, she rushed into speech.

'Have you any of Brian Lane's patients in there? I could shower and change into respectable clothes and come with you.'

Shower with Will in the house?

'Or better still meet you at the hospital. Dad's car will be in the garage.'

He didn't reply, though frown lines appeared on his forehead as he studied her.

'You don't have to do that,' he said. 'Even if you intended starting with Brian immediately, you wouldn't be expected in before Monday. Have a rest, relax, enjoy being close to your river again.'

Alex turned the boat back into the main river, heading for home. She could hardly tell Will that she didn't want to be alone in the house, because it was more than that. For some reason, although for years she'd not only enjoyed but had treasured her own company, right now she was—

Afraid of it?

Not exactly.

More afraid of how she'd react to it in these totally different circumstances and without the father she'd come home to get to know.

You've already proved to him what a wimp you are, asking him to walk through the rooms with you, so don't make it worse. You're better than that! Stronger! she told herself.

'You're right,' she said out loud, 'especially as there's so much to do here. And I don't officially start with Brian's group for another fortnight. I thought I'd need that long at home with Dad while he got over the op.'

Did her voice quaver that Will reached out and touched her knee?

Whatever! The touch reminded her of all the reasons she *shouldn't* be spending more time with Will. A man with a child needed stability in his life—or in the child's life at least. How could she, with her record of broken relationships, provide that?

'I'm only a phone call away,' he was saying. 'If you need anything, anything at all, give me a call. My home and mobile numbers are with the papers I left in your living room. Seriously, Alex, I want you to know I'm here for you if ever you need a hand.'

Did that sound pathetic? Will wondered, sitting back and studying the woman who was steering the little tinnie up onto the beach outside her father's house.

He helped her slide the boat onto the trailer and wheel it back up into place beneath the house.

No excuse now for lingering, although every cell in his body was suggesting lingering wasn't all it wanted from this woman.

'Well, I'll be off, but do yell if you need me,' he said, as Alex busied herself taking the fuel tank out of the boat and storing it away.

She finished the task and came to stand beside him.

'You could live to regret that offer,' she said, a smile lighting up her eyes, although her face seemed sombre. 'You're probably the only person in town willing to talk to me.'

'You can't mean that!' he said. 'All that business was fifteen years ago—more like twenty, in fact—who'd remember?'

Now the smile touched her lips but not convincingly.

'Only all my parents' friends. It's worse now Dad has died. The talk will be I came home to grab whatever he's left behind.'

'But your own friends, surely there'd be someone—'

'Who didn't blame me for the sainted Mr Spencer being exposed for what he was? I was at a church school—all my friends were from the school. Once the jury said not guilty I was branded as a whore who slept around and used Mr Spencer as a scapegoat when things got difficult.'

'But—'

The smile had gone, replaced by a look of such weariness he wanted to hold her in his arms and comfort her as he would have one of the twins.

'Even my friends who believed it was Mr Spencer thought it was my fault—I must have led him on, that kind of thing. To most of them, to a lot of people, the man was a saint.'

She gave a tiny shrug—a bare lift of the shoulders— and tried another smile, this one so pathetic he did take her in his arms and hold her close, a hug, nothing more…

Although—

'So why stay here, now your father's gone?'

She eased out of his arms and looked, not at him but out across the river.

'It is my home,' she whispered, 'and the river is in my heart. I did no wrong, so why should I be driven away from what I love?'

Will heard the strength back in her voice, saw it in the now upright stance, and felt like clapping. She had guts, the kid he'd known all that time ago—the kid who had grown into this beautiful woman and brought such confusion into his life the instant he'd set eyes on her again.

'I'll talk to you later,' he said, knowing he had to get away and sort out the confusion. He'd go home—where he should be—and play with Charlotte.

Now!

He was surprised by how early it was when he arrived home. Charlotte was up but still in her pyjamas, the cereal she'd had for breakfast sprinkled liberally down her top.

'She's all yours,' his mother said, but when she held out her arms to give Charlotte a hug, although the little girl was only going through an ever-open door to another part of the house, Will saw the love between the two of them and was reassured that his mother wasn't regretting her offer.

'I can't stay long, Daddy,' Charlotte told him as he peeled off her pyjamas. 'Nani and I are going to a party later.'

'A party?'

Vague memories stirred in his head but so much had happened since late yesterday afternoon he couldn't catch the right one.

'It's on the fridge,' Charlotte told him, dashing naked to the refrigerator to pull off a garish party invitation. 'Chloe's party!'

Answers clicked into place. Chloe was the grand-daughter of his mother's best friend and the two children played together often.

'Nani and me bought her a present—we bought her a fairy doll that flies. Can I have one too, Daddy?'

He lifted his daughter, tucked her under one arm and carried her shrieking to the bathroom for a quick wash and a good teeth clean.

'Maybe for your birthday,' he said, wondering just what kind of toy a fairy that flew might be. He'd have to check it out.

She ran ahead of him into her bedroom, and, watching the small, naked form, he felt a heart-crunching sense of love mingled with the fear that he knew all parents must feel—fear that something bad might happen to her.

'Are we going to the park?' she asked, sitting on the floor pulling on her undies. 'Or the beach?'

'Which would you like?' he asked, although he knew the answer. She'd just discovered she could swing on the monkey bars at the park, although he held a little of her weight as she shifted from hand to hand, and was ready to catch her at any moment.

'Okay, park,' he agreed, when she gave the expected answer, 'but do you need two skirts?'

It was an argument he wasn't going to win. The daughter he'd thought of as a tomboy for her first three years had suddenly gone girly and now wore frilly skirts, the frillier the better, one on top of another.

Then came the serious business of choosing a top. She delved through her drawers in search of the one with the most spangles on it.

He said a silent prayer of thanks that his mother kept Charlotte's 'good' clothes in her unit, so would be able to sort an outfit for the party.

But pushing her on the swing, altering the words of a monkey song *he'd* learned at kindergarten to 'when Charlotte Ke-ent has a swing' with her pointing her toes to the air instead of a monkey tail around a branch, he usually felt a sense of contentment.

Charlotte loved the swing and insisted on the song, but, unfortunately, pushing a swing, even while singing, was a mindless operation, and his mind drifted to Alex's return into the ambit of his life.

Common sense said back away, he had Charlotte to consider, but Alex was already so isolated he couldn't do that.

He could be there for her while she settled in and made new friends, then ease away.

Ease away—that was a laugh.

'Daddy, it's a magpie.'

He realised from Charlotte's tone it wasn't the first time she'd pointed the bird out to him, so he shut the door on the part of his brain already too overloaded with Alex and concentrated on his daughter, moving from swings to the slippery slide and finally the monkey bars.

Will had hurried away, striding up the side of the house as if all the furies in hell had been chasing him. Alex had watched him go, bemused by his sudden departure, but at the same time glad he'd gone so she could sit down somewhere quiet and try to work out exactly what emotion Will Kent had awoken in her body.

And now she thought about it, *that* was something she *had* to do alone.

The phone was ringing as she walked back into the house, and her immediate reaction was to ignore it, but she'd been a doctor too long to ignore a ringing phone, so she lifted the receiver and said her name, hoping she sounded more positive than she felt.

'Anthony Mitchell here…' The caller hesitated and Alex realised he wasn't sure how to address her. 'I'm the dean of medicine at Heritage University. I want to offer my sincere condolences on your father's death.'

Slightly surprised, Alex thanked him, and was wondering just why he might be phoning when he continued.

'I'm not sure if you've been told but he donated his body to the university. I'd like to call in and see you some time to discuss your father's generous gift and to explain how we go about things. I realise this is a very tough time for you, but—'

Alex could hear the embarrassment in the man's voice and guessed he wanted to see her as soon as possible.

'I could see you today,' she said, to save him further discomfort. 'Do you want me to come to you, or what?'

'No, no, I wouldn't ask that of you. I'll come to you. Say half an hour?'

Half an hour to find some respectable clothes, have a shower—

'That would be fine,' she heard herself say.

A few polite farewells, and the conversation was done.

Alex closed her eyes and breathed deeply. This was good, it's getting back to normal, she told herself, heading up the stairs to rifle through her suitcases for something suitable for entertaining the dean!

* * *

Her first impression was that deans hadn't looked like that when she'd been at university. Or maybe her being younger had made them look older.

Walking up the path was a tall, fair-haired, fortyish man in pale chinos, a dark blue T-shirt and sandals.

Closer up he was definitely unlike any dean she'd ever seen. Alex had a quiet bet with herself that more young women than young men would enrol in medicine simply to be taught by him.

'Anthony Mitchell,' the dean with a distinct resemblance to a Greek god said, offering his hand. 'Actually, it's Tony—much easier.'

Alex took the offered hand and introduced herself, also using the shortened version of *her* name.

'Come through, I've tea or coffee, or a cold drink if you'd prefer. We'll sit out on the deck, if that's okay with you.'

'More than okay,' Tony replied. 'I live in an apartment overlooking the ocean but I've often wondered about these houses along the river. Wow!'

They'd reached the deck, and his exclamation of appreciation made Alex warm to him.

'The view's so peaceful in spite of all the activity on the river,' he said. 'I bet you used to sit out here for hours as a kid.'

Alex smiled at his enthusiasm.

'More like out there, looking back,' she said. 'I had a tinnie from the time I was five. I grew up on the river.'

She was about to ask what she could get him when Buddy joined the party, his shrieking 'Where's Bruce' startling the visitor, who stepped back in surprise.

'Sorry,' Alex said. 'That's Buddy. He's a little uncontrolled and before you ask, no, we never knew where he got the name Bruce or who Bruce might have been, let alone where he is at any given time.'

Tony laughed and held out his hand to the bird, who studied it for a while, before choosing to perch on the railing.

At least Buddy had broken any awkwardness, and now, when Alex offered a drink, Tony settled on coffee, also offering to help.

'No, sit and admire the view,' Alex told him, mostly because she didn't want a stranger in the kitchen when she was still, in some ways, trying to find her own way around it.

The coffee was easy and instinct took her to the big pantry and the pile of cake tins always kept on the middle shelf.

Only one remained, but when Alex lifted it she felt the weight.

Could it be?

She opened the tin to find, as she'd half expected, the treacly aroma of Anzac biscuits wafting out at her.

Swallowing hard, she put some biscuits on a plate, put milk and sugar, small plates and napkins on a tray, and carried it out to set it on the table in front of the dean.

Tony!

Returning with the coffeepot, she found him munching on a biscuit.

'Home-made Anzacs, I thought you'd just got back from overseas.'

Another swallow, and a quick sniff back of tears, hopefully unnoticed as Buddy swooped to take a biscuit from the plate.

'My mother was the baker in the family—cakes, slices, biscuits—but my dad always made the Anzacs. He said because his father was a dinkum Anzac who had landed at Gallipoli, he was the only one entitled to make the biscuits. He must have made these before he went into hospital.'

Sniffing and swallowing was no longer enough and Alex excused herself, heading for the house so she could wipe away the evidence of the completely unexpected emotion she was feeling.

But Tony was up before her, sliding an arm around her shoulders.

'I'm sorry—it's far too soon to be having to tackle stuff like this. Some guy at the hospital told me the sooner I got it over and done with the better, but I can go away and come back another day. Have you someone to stay with you? A friend?'

A friend?

It was a logical question for how could someone who'd grown up in this town come home to no one?

Although there *was* Caitlin...

If she was still around...

'I'll be fine,' Alex assured her visitor, easing away from his solid, comforting body. 'It's silly because I've been, well, separated, I suppose you'd say, from my family for nearly twenty years, then something like my dad's Anzac biscuits make me cry. But I'm okay now. Sit down and have your coffee and another biscuit, and tell me what I need to do to finalise things for the university.'

She'd thought she'd sounded very together, but Tony was eyeing her somewhat dubiously, although he did sit and sip at his coffee.

'If you're sure you're up to it,' he said.

'I am,' Alex said firmly, but was nearly overwhelmed again when Buddy flew to sit on her shoulder.

She had *one* friend.

Two, if she could find Caitlin, her childhood best friend.

Three, if she counted Will.

But maybe she shouldn't count Will.

Tony was talking about the river and a group at the university—mainly medical-school staff—who'd formed a kayaking club and had fortnightly outings on the river, and once a month a trip away to some other river to try the rapids or paddle across estuaries.

'You'd be more than welcome to join,' he said, and as Alex was about to reply that she didn't have a kayak—and didn't have very good balance in the ones she'd tried— she realised it was a good way to meet people socially.

'That sounds fun,' she said. 'Perhaps you could give me details.'

'Better than that,' Tony told her. 'Our monthly meeting is next Thursday evening. I could pick you up and take you, maybe have dinner later—a group of us often go on.'

Had his original invitation sounded too much like a date? Alex wondered, but, group or not, she needed to be doing something with her spare time, and maybe meeting other men—other than Will, that was—because the Will thing was just too confusing...

'I'd love it,' she said, and realised she meant it. It was just the thing she needed to help her settle back into the town, and doing anything on the river would be fun.

They finally got down to the paperwork, Tony explaining that her father had expressed his wish that no memorial service be held.

'He wanted a minimum of fuss,' Tony told her, 'although that wouldn't stop you having a few of his friends and relations around if you wished. He made all the arrangements himself, and it really only needs one signature from you, acknowledging that we're taking the body. Virtually signing him over to us.'

Alex signed, although she couldn't help but wonder what had prompted her father to do this. She was a listed organ donor herself, and later intended willing her body to a university, but it seemed such an alien thing for her father to have done.

'Did he ever say why?' she asked Tony, who looked slightly startled by the question.

'I never asked him,' he said. 'I suppose I just assumed it was because you'd studied medicine and he felt he was doing his bit. He talked about you a lot. I know he was very proud of you.'

Hmm!

Alex tucked that thought away to consider some other time, and agreed she'd be ready for the Thursday meeting if Tony collected her at six.

'Though it's probably better if I take my car—that way, if we're late you won't get stuck here when the ferry stops.'

He shrugged. 'I can always get home around by the highway. It's a bit further but not a worry. And the place where we meet is tricky to find the first time. I'll see you at six.'

With which he walked through the house with her, shook her hand, and departed.

CHAPTER FOUR

ALEX WALKED BACK into the house, aware her clothes were scattered in the upstairs hall, knowing she had to unpack—to sort things out—but totally lost as to where to start.

Presumably the house was now her house. In fact, it wasn't a presumption, her father had told her the details of his will—'everything to my daughter Alexandra', as simple as that. So it *was* her house, although it felt very alien right now. Apart from the kitchen and the deck, which definitely felt like home.

But her old bedroom?

Her father's room?

Could she live in either?

The sewing room!

For some reason, when she'd walked through the house with Will she hadn't thought to enter the sewing room.

Because it had been so much her mother's domain?

Because she'd feared it would be as much changed as her parents' bedroom?

Well, no time like the present…

She stepped over clothes and suitcases to open the door at the end of the hall—the door to the room that looked out over the roof of the deck to the river. Here her mother's long sewing desk had been built in so she could sew and see the river at the same time.

Alex's hand hesitated on the doorknob as she wondered, for the first time, why her parents hadn't made this room—the room with the view—their bedroom?

She opened the door and almost closed it again, the transformation was so startling. Gone was the long bench and the cabinets that had held cloth and cotton; gone was the serviceable felt carpet that had covered the floor; gone were the shutters her mother would lower over the windows when the setting sun peeked in.

In their place were a brand-new bedroom suite, the bed clothed in the softest of grey linens, a polished timber floor, sleek blinds that rolled down to keep out the glare but not hide the view, and sitting in the middle of the bed the threadbare galah that had been Alex's favourite toy even before the advent of Buddy.

Down the far end was a door and, opening it, Alex found a tiny en suite bathroom, grey with touches of pink, just like the bedroom colours.

Tears streamed down her face as she considered the amount of work her father must have done to transform this room for her. And regret that it had been so long, that she'd not come home sooner, that they'd lost so many years together, all gathered in her chest like a physical pain.

She sank down on the bed, hugging her misery to herself, rocking as she cried out the pain of the lost years.

Will hadn't intended visiting. In fact, his intention had been to see as little as possible of Alex until he'd sorted out how he felt about her. But after Brian's phone call he knew it would be better to talk to her in person. That way, he could, hopefully, gauge if she was ready to start work earlier than planned—emotionally, and also physically, given the long plane trip—or if he should advise Brian to get a locum.

So, with his mother and Charlotte off at their party, he drove to the house and rang the bell.

No reply.

He checked the car was in the garage, and the boat in the shed beneath the house.

He rang the bell again, called her name, then began to get anxious about her.

She'd been through so much emotional turmoil in such a short time...

Buddy's arrival from the back of the house—an agitated Buddy—tightened Will's tension and banished any doubts about entering the house.

He found the rock that hid the key and opened the door, Buddy bouncing on his shoulder, enquiring about Bruce.

'Forget Bruce, where's Alex?' Will muttered at the bird, who cocked his head as if considering the question, then flew off through the house, swooping back to land on the banister at the top of the stairs.

'I'm not stupid enough to follow you without at least looking down here,' Will told him, walking swiftly through the lower rooms and checking the deck.

Buddy had moved and was lifting pieces of Alex's clothing in his beak, making more of a mess of the upstairs hall than had probably been there in the beginning. Although the chaos of half-unpacked suitcases made Will's heart beat faster.

He checked the first room—the monastic room of her father—empty.

Checked the next, the Alex schoolgirl room—also empty.

It was only as he shut the door he noticed another door at the end of the hall—a room they hadn't entered earlier.

Why? he wondered, but as Buddy was now jumping up and down on the doorknob, Will approached it, calling to Alex, although softly this time.

She was asleep on the bed, her arms wrapped around her body and something that looked like a very dead bird. Tearstains on her cheeks tugged at Will's heart as he stood looking down at her.

She was breathing, she was okay, he should let her sleep, and although he knew he couldn't stand there, looking at her, he was reluctant to leave.

Buddy solved the problem, bouncing up and down on Alex's head with his raucous cry of 'Who's a pretty girl, then?'

Her eyes opened slowly—blue as the late afternoon sky beyond the windows.

'I'm sorry for intruding, I had a message for you and you didn't answer the door and—'

'It's okay,' she said sleepily. 'I don't know why I fell asleep. I should be up—there's stuff to do.'

She sat up on the bed, looking around in unmistakeable wonder.

'My father did this for me,' she whispered to him. 'He did all this and I didn't know. I didn't look in here this morning—too many memories, I suppose—but he's transformed it, made this beautiful room with the river right there...'

And the tears came again.

He'd have had to be made of marble to have not reacted, Will realised as he sat beside her on the bed and put his arm around her, drawing her close to offer comfort.

'You've had a rough homecoming,' he said quietly. 'You're entitled to a good cry.'

'Not really,' she protested, easing a little apart but remaining in the circle of his arm. 'I don't know why I'm being such a wuss.'

'Such a wuss, such a wuss!' the bird shrieked, and Alex recovered completely.

'Buddy, you've learned new words!' She stared at the bird in amazement, truly surprised but very thankful for the diversion, because being held by Will was far too enticing and she'd been battling an urge to snuggle closer.

'Give me a minute, I'll meet you out on the deck,' she said.

She'd been about to add that they could watch the sunset when she realised that might not be a good idea. Too much romance in joint sunset watching…

He walked away and she eased herself off the bed, hurried into the little bathroom and splashed water on her face, brushed her tousled hair.

Will had said something about a message.

Presumably for her.

Get downstairs and ask him, she told herself, for all she'd have preferred not to have seen Will quite so soon.

Not until she'd sorted out a few things in her head—and body—and preferably not until she'd gone to the kayaking meeting and met people and had at least the beginnings of a normal social life.

As if that would help! the cynic in her head whispered.

Ignoring it, she headed downstairs, joining her visitor on the deck as the setting sun painted the western sky with extravagantly brilliant red and purple and orange streaks.

She shook her head at the beauty of it and refused to give way to tears again. Instead, she plonked down in a chair out of touching distance from Will and said brightly, 'A message?'

He studied her for a moment, as if assessing her current emotional state—or perhaps her ability to understand a message.

'Brian Lane phoned. He'd heard about your father's death and someone had told him I'd seen you at the hospital so I think he wanted me to suss out how you were—how your father's death had affected you.'

'Because?' Alex asked, aware she was frowning but unable to guess where this conversation was going.

Did the man she was going to work with think she might be too emotionally fragile to handle the work?

'Because he'd like you to start earlier if you could,' Will told her. 'He's in Melbourne, where he's trying to arrange care for his mother, who has dementia, and he's having a tough time finding somewhere suitable. His wife's got three children under four so she stayed at home, but Brian really needs more time down there.'

'And the other partner? Mal Parker?'

'Is booked to fly to the US on Tuesday for a conference. He could cancel, but Brian phoned me to ask what I thought. It's not a frantically busy practice—two practitioners can handle it easily. I don't know if Brian told you, but apparently his aim in taking you on was so he could return to Melbourne, where both his and his wife's families live.'

'So it normally has two doctors, but one can manage?' Alex asked, as she took in what Will was telling her and realised that starting work would be the best possible thing for her in the circumstances. Especially if she was busy!

'That's right. The practice manager will sort out the appointments so you're not overwhelmed but they had already planned to have only one doctor there for the next fortnight so it shouldn't take too much fiddling.'

Will stopped and looked at her expectantly.

'What do you think?'

What did she think, apart from how his eyes seemed to be saying things that weren't coming out in his words?

Worrying about her?

Forget the man's eyes!

'I'm happy to do it. It will be good to have something to do—something to keep me busy while I settle back into the town. But I need to speak to Brian myself, and maybe arrange to go into the rooms tomorrow. I wonder if I could get the practice manager to meet me there to show me around and explain how they do things.'

'I'm sure Brian can arrange it, and I have his number here if you want to phone him now.'

Will pulled out his mobile and scrolled through it, finally coming up with what he was looking for. He passed her the phone, their fingers touching, electricity jolting through Alex for all the transaction was purely business.

She carried the phone inside to write down the number—*and* to get away from the distraction that was Will. Her reactions to him were nothing more than by-products of the emotional storm she'd come home to, she told herself as she jotted down the number.

They had to be because they were like nothing she'd ever felt before.

Will had joined her in the kitchen.

'Mum and Charlotte are eating out so what if I go down to the co-op while you're talking to Brian and get us fish and chips for tea? I'm sure it's the proper homecoming dinner to eat on your deck.'

Fish and chips on the deck!

Twenty years ago it had been a Sunday evening treat because her mother had never cooked on a Sunday. Sunday had been a day for church in the morning, and reading or playing quietly in her room in the afternoon. Her parents, with their strong beliefs, had spent Sunday afternoons studying their Bibles. As an adult, Alex had often wondered why they had found it so hard to apply its teachings about love and forgiveness to their own daughter.

But fish and chips on the deck would be a true homecoming. They had always been the best part of long, slow Sundays.

'Sounds lovely,' she said, ignoring all the alarm bells about Will and proximity that were going off in her head. After all, she'd need someone to talk to about the job she was to start on Monday, and Will would probably know something of the set-up in the practice.

Business, purely business, she reminded herself.

Brian was delighted to hear from her, offered his sympathies, thanked her effusively and promised to get Marilyn, the practice manager, to phone as soon as possible.

'I'm sure she'll be only too happy to spend time with you tomorrow, because we all owe you a huge debt for this.'

Strangely at ease now that decision had been made, Alex returned to the deck, where the more muted colours of the dying sunset were just as beautiful a sight.

Tomorrow, learning about the practice, then on Monday the excitement of starting a new job would banish all the other strange emotional stuff that had been going on in her head since her father's death and the weird physical stuff going on in her body since meeting Will again, and soon she'd have a whole new life in the town she'd once called home.

She'd brought the handset of the phone out onto the deck with her, and the ringtone startled her out of her dreams of a new life.

Sure it would be Marilyn, she answered with her name, then listened in shock as a woman's voice screamed into her ear.

'You ruined my life, you slut!' the voice said, then the caller slammed the phone down.

Alex stared at the slim piece of plastic that had delivered the message—stared warily as one would at a snake or perhaps a poisonous spider.

It had to be a wrong number, and the woman hadn't listened when she'd said her name.

That would explain it.

But the venom in the voice had unsettled her.

Fortunately, the next phone call—and, yes, she was a doctor, she'd *had* to answer it—was Marilyn, so a sensible conversation about where and when to meet the following day pushed the ugly words to the back of Alex's mind.

Will's return was another diversion—a confusing diversion but right now confusion was better than mulling over the phone call.

Seeing her there, with the river behind her reflecting the fading colours of the sunset, Will wondered how he could not fall in love with her.

If only love wasn't off limits—too hard, too hurtful—and then there was Charlotte...

'Fish and chips for two,' he said, far too brightly, 'and a bottle of a nice sav blanc to go with them. I should have asked what you'd like. I just thought...'

He was behaving like a schoolboy with his first crush on a girl, except this girl was a woman, and a beautiful one at that, and he wasn't sure...

Well, in truth, he wasn't sure what he wasn't sure about, although deep down he knew it was to do with

Charlotte and her well-being, and love, love lost, and pain...

'Sounds great. I'll get us glasses—and do you want plates or will we eat them out of the paper?'

Ah, something he *was* sure about.

'I think they taste best out of the paper.'

She grinned at him.

'Me, too!'

Yet for all the light-hearted chat, he sensed a tension in the air.

Sexual tension?

Yes, some of that! Inevitable from his point of view whenever he was near Alex.

But something else as well.

She returned with not only glasses but an ice bucket as well, set them on the table, then poured the wine before propping the bottle in the bucket amidst the ice.

She smiled again.

'You know, I imagine this is the very first time that the ice bucket has held anything alcoholic. My parents got it for a wedding present, and I remember at Christmas they'd get a bottle of non-alcoholic wine from the supermarket and the ice bucket would be set in pride of place in the middle of the table.'

Maybe he was imagining her tension, he decided as he smiled at her little tale and carefully unwrapped enough of the parcel of food for them to begin eating.

'Did you speak to Marilyn?'

Alex nodded around the end of a very long chip.

'She can't do tomorrow morning so I'm meeting her at two in the afternoon. She sounds very nice.'

'She is,' Will replied, 'and one of the most efficient practice managers I've ever met. She runs those rooms like a military operation yet everyone loves her and is happy to have her yell at them when things don't go according to plan.'

'Does she yell very often?' Alex asked.

'Only at the doctors,' Will assured her. 'They *will* run over their appointment times and ruin her timetables!'

Alex laughed.

'Every practice needs a Marilyn,' she said, seemingly at ease, yet again Will sensed there was something bothering her.

Was the attraction he was feeling not one-sided? Was Alex feeling something towards him but conflicted over it because he knew her from the past?

Or *his* past?

Heaven knew, he felt weirdly disloyal towards Elise for the way he was feeling, so perhaps—

'Grave thoughts?' she said, startling him out of his meandering imaginings.

'Stupid thoughts,' he countered, determined to put all the attraction stuff aside. 'Brian said one of the reasons he was pleased to appoint you to the team was that you were happy to assist in operations.'

It wasn't quite a question but she took it as one.

'I love being involved when my patients go to Theatre. I worked in a private hospital in Glasgow so often worked on the surgeon's team. I tossed up doing surgery, but I like patient contact and felt I wouldn't get enough as a surgeon.'

Nice, easy, medical conversation, and he had to be imagining the thread of tension in her voice.

Most likely tiredness, exhaustion even, given her recent arrival and the stress that had followed it.

Alex wasn't sure how long she could sit there, eating chips and chatting away to Will when the echoes of the phone call were still ringing in her head.

But much as she longed to tell him, she knew she couldn't keep leaning on him for support, especially when the attraction she was feeling towards him showed no sign of abating.

So they talked of work, of patients they'd had, and finally of a young lad who would be her patient.

'He's seventeen, with congenital heart problems that have got beyond salvage, so he's waiting for a donor heart.'

'Would someone do it here?' Alex asked, surprised, although organ transplant techniques were now so advanced most major hospitals could cope with them.

'If a suitable donor turned up, yes. Ideally, he should be in a capital city while he waits, but it could be months.'

'Or even longer, and he'd be away from his friends and family and in the end it could all be for nothing,' Alex finished, and Will nodded.

'Brian and the cardiovascular surgeon have both backed him wanting to stay here, sure it's better for him to grab whatever happiness he can, but I worry sometimes that it was the right decision.'

'You've got the facilities and personnel?'

'To do either a harvest operation or the transplant, yes, but if the heart was here, we'd have to bring in a team of surgeons to do the harvest. That's already been set up, with cardiovascular people prepared to fly in, but it's more likely the heart would be somewhere else, and it would be harvested where the donor is and then flown here.'

The idea that she might be involved in a transplant sent a different kind of thrill through Alex's body.

Good, this was good. Getting excited about work would soon stop her getting excited about Will.

Perhaps, she added ruefully to herself as he smiled at her and it was obvious the other thrill was still there.

But it *had* diverted her from the phone call, which she was now prepared to put down to a wrong number.

So they talked of work, sipped wine, and ate their fish and chips. The talking of work part was okay, but watching Will take a sip of wine—he took very few sips, his glass still half-full—or his lips close around a morsel of fish was flustering, to say the least.

Darkness had fallen on the river, so it had taken on a silver sheen, and occasional soft shushing sounds as ripples from a passing craft washed ashore somehow made the scene even more peaceful.

He should go!

Will knew that as well as he knew his name.

But sitting here with Alex was as close to total relaxation as he'd felt in a long time.

Almost total relaxation.

She was taking a sip of wine, and even in the gloom he could make out her lips closing on the glass—full, sensual lips…

He imagined them closing on his mouth, sipping—

Body hardening, he pushed away his glass, stood, and gathered up the paper wrappings, tipping out one last, cold chip.

'Want it?' he said, holding it out to Alex, aware he was using it as an excuse to touch her fingers, equally aware he had to sort out his feelings before this went any further.

Buddy saved the day, swooping from his perch on the railing, where he'd been quietly scolding some errant seagulls.

'Too late,' Alex said, laughing at the antics of the bird as she too rose to her feet.

Close enough to touch, to reach out and draw her into his arms.

She was close enough to touch him and a treacherous voice in her head suggested if she told him of the phone call he'd do the touching—he'd hold her to comfort her—but this whole situation was too…false? Artificial? Too *something*.

She'd come home to her father's death and Will had been there for her—Will was the only familiar person in the town she once had known, but wasn't it too easy to confuse comfort for something more personal?

But she *did* take the wrappings from him, aware it was probably an excuse to touch his fingers!

Leading the way back through the house, she thanked him for bringing Brian's message and explaining so much of the set-up she'd be going into.

Did she sound as stilted and formal to him as she did to herself?

Maybe, for he grinned and gave a little bow.

'My pleasure, Dr Hudson,' he said.

She smiled.

'You can call me Alex,' she replied teasingly.

And was startled when he said, in a surprisingly deep and serious tone, 'I would like that very much, Alex.'

Upon which he kissed her cheek and was gone.

'I will not press my hand to where he kissed me,' Alex muttered to herself, scrunching the chip wrapping tighter so her fingers wouldn't stray.

But as she went upstairs, stepping over the chaos of clothes still littering the hall, to go into the new bedroom, she couldn't help but wonder if she'd ever get to share the beauty of this special room with someone special.

Special like Will?

She thrust away the thought and busied herself putting

clothes from the hall and her second suitcase into her new wardrobes, setting out her toiletries in her new bathroom.

It's the beginning of a whole new life, she reminded herself, and it's up to you to make the most of it.

But not alone, her heart protested, not alone...

CHAPTER FIVE

SUNDAY MORNING AND Alex luxuriated in the comfortable new bed, lying there, looking out at her beloved river. She thought of the past, the life she'd once had, here by the river—of her mother, who'd been unable to comfort her when she'd needed it and had died without forgiving her for a sin she hadn't committed.

Long ago, with help from counsellors, she'd forgiven her mother's behaviour, aware that if she hadn't taken that step it would have poisoned her life.

But her father?

What had *he* been thinking when he'd made this room for her?

Regret?

He'd asked for forgiveness and she'd given it whole-heartedly, but this gift spoke of love.

'Love' hadn't been a word much used in her home— apart from love for God. Although Alex had felt loved when she and her father had been out in the tinnie, when he'd held her hand to steady it while she'd baited a hook...

Was that what love was?

A steadying hand?

Now she grieved for the man who'd held it out to her, setting aside the pain of his later rejection.

And sorrow that she hadn't had more time to spend

with him—time to tell him all was well—almost swamped her.

It's hunger, she told herself, and left the warm nest of her bed.

Her father had stocked up on basics but it was obvious she'd have to shop, especially as she was starting work the next day, and shopping time in future might be severely restricted.

Time to take her father's car out of the garage.

Wondering why she hadn't even bothered to check what kind of vehicle it was, she found the keys hanging where they had always hung, used the automatic door-opener to open the garage then went out and blinked in surprise at her father's choice of vehicle—a fairly new, bright red, small SUV.

Red! Like the car she'd been saving up for all those years ago, although back then all she'd wanted had been something small and cheap!

But what fun to have this to run around in, was her next thought, then guilt that she wasn't feeling worse about her father's death damped down the pleasure.

Although, she thought, she now understood enough of her father's thinking not to get too depressed.

The bedroom, this smart new *red* car—these were his way of saying he was sorry—of making restitution for the lost years, which made it okay to take pleasure in his unexpected gifts.

Didn't it?

She shook her head, nearly as confused over her father renewing contact as she was over Will.

Think shopping, not Will!

Marilyn proved every bit as pleasant and efficient as Will had said, and Alex knew she'd soon settle into the routine of the practice. She'd been there for two hours and was going through the patient list for the week when the pager Marilyn had presented to Alex buzzed.

'It's the hospital,' Marilyn told her, as Alex lifted the phone to make the call.

She listened as a nurse explained the problem then hung up and turned to Marilyn.

'Do you know a Mr Miller—Peter Miller?'

'Unstable AF,' Marilyn said succinctly. 'Brian had been hoping his heart had settled down but if he's in hospital it's playing up again. He knows to take his pulse every day and to head straight for the hospital if he goes into fibrillation so I guess your welcome to Port will be a cardioversion.'

'Can you get his file for me, please?' Alex asked, wanting to know as much about the patient as she could before she met him.

Marilyn returned, handing it to Alex and adding, 'Do you want me to let the ICU know we'll need someone to do the anaesthetic for you?'

'I suppose so, if that's the procedure, although perhaps we should call Mal Parker.'

Marilyn shook her head.

'He'd be happy to come—Mr Easygoing, that's Mal— but I think you should do it—plunge right in—then nothing will seem as strange later. You'll meet some of the hospital staff and begin to know your way around and it'll give you confidence in starting the new job.'

Alex nodded, but she wasn't quite sure about Marilyn's theory. In fact, she was beginning to feel a little overwhelmed—too big an information dump in too short a time, and now this...

The procedure itself was simple and usually a nurse with cardiac training would set it all up—could probably do it—so all the doctor had to do was wait until the patient was anaesthetised then turn the switch to deliver an electric charge to shock the heart back into normal rhythm.

But in a strange hospital, with a new anaesthetist— and she didn't even know where the patient would be.

Not that she wouldn't manage.

'Will Kent is on call at the hospital this weekend,' Marilyn said. 'I've phoned him to come in.'

'Will Kent? But he's an intensivist,' Alex protested, not at all sure she was ready to see Will again.

'Well,' Marilyn replied, 'that's who does all the small anaesthesia jobs at the hospital. Intensivists are trained in practically everything.'

'Of course!' Alex said, still trying to get to grips with the fact she'd be working with Will on her first job in the hospital. 'Well, I'll go and see Mr Miller, find out when he first noticed it. We've got twenty-four hours, thirty at a pinch, to safely do the shock treatment, and if there's any doubt he can go onto drugs for a month and have it then.'

Marilyn nodded approvingly, and Alex headed for the hospital, Mr Miller's file tucked under her arm.

At least, she thought as she crossed the road to the hospital building, she knew the way to the coronary care ward as it was on the same floor as the ICU where her father had been.

Atrial fibrillation—the offset beat of the patient's atrium—could cause blood clots to come loose from the wall of the heart, blocking arteries, leading to strokes—

The information buzzed in her head.

But every hospital was different, so—

Thud!

Of course it had to be Will she'd run into—Will who

held her shoulders to steady her, Will who smiled down into her eyes.

'Going somewhere?' he asked, the twinkle in his eyes sending tremors through her body.

'First patient.'

She blurted out the words, her thoughts swooping between the procedure and how solid Will's chest had felt when she'd hit it.

'Then we'll go together,' he said, the hint of laughter in his voice echoing that twinkle. 'Did Marilyn tell you I'm doing the anaesthetic?'

She looked directly at him now, and sighed.

'Is that so bad?' he asked, the laughter still there.

'No,' she muttered at him, not wanting to reveal that she'd been kind of hoping for a few Will-free hours so she could try to sort out her reactions to him.

Had he sensed her reluctance that he said, 'We could get Mal in to do it.'

She glared at the man who had brought unnecessary complications into her life. 'I haven't spoken to the patient but it sounds like a straightforward cardioversion. A monkey with a bit of training could do it so I really think I can manage.'

'Ah, but as well as the monkey?' Will teased, falling into step beside her. 'Anyway, at least I can introduce you to some of the staff, and tell you all the gossip about them, and help you fit right in.'

Alex sighed.

She wasn't exactly flustered but Will's presence was having its usual unsettling effect and the one thing she didn't need when she was working was any kind of distraction.

But it was impossible to argue. She needed an anaesthetist and he was, apparently, it.

They were already at the nurses' station in the coronary care ward and he was introducing her as Brian's new recruit.

'He's been held up in Melbourne so Alex will be taking over his patients, who include...'

He finally stopped talking and turned to Alex.

'Peter Miller,' she said.

'Oh, good,' the nurse answered. 'Can you do him now? It's just that he managed to get through this afternoon's milking and if you can zap him tonight he can stay a few hours then get back home in time for morning milking.'

'Not a problem I encountered in Glasgow,' Alex said, smiling at the thought of a procedure needing to be scheduled around milking time, but the hinterland of this town was famous dairy country.

A nurse led her into a large private room, where her patient was lying on the bed, chatting to another nurse, who was checking the monitor leads taped to his body. Alex introduced herself to Peter and asked him about his symptoms, at the same time reading the information the monitor was providing. His pulse was running at just over a hundred and twenty—jumping between that and a low of ninety, and the hospital information board told her he'd had drugs to slow it and also an injection to thin his blood.

In the corner of the room was a bulky but efficient shock-treatment machine, with leads set out ready to be attached to pads on Peter's skin.

'Two years since last time,' Peter was telling her. 'The nurse says it's good to have gone that long.'

'It is indeed,' Alex told him.

She flicked through his file to the last cardioversion to check if he'd had any adverse reactions but, no, he'd been fine.

By the time she looked up a small crowd had gathered at the door.

'Not much happens around here,' Will said, 'so they're curious about the new doctor.'

'Well, that's a pity because the show's over for them. We need to shut the door.'

The small crowd at the door melted away as the CCU nurse went towards them.

Concentrating now on her work, Alex checked Peter's weight so she could set the correct charge, watched as the nurse stuck the rectangular pads into place, one onto his chest close to his left nipple and the other opposite it on his back. Once Peter was settled, Will put an oxygen mask over his nose and mouth, asked the nurse to hold it, and slid a catheter into the back of their patient's hand.

It was a swift procedure, a small amount of drug, the nod from Will, a single charge—Peter's body lifting slightly off the bed—then all eyes went to the monitor to see if the heart had reverted to a normal beat.

'Well done,' Will said to her, and although it could have sounded patronising, Alex took it as the praise it was.

'It was a fairly simple start to my Heritage Port career,' Alex told him.

'But good to get it over with?'

He smiled as she spoke and the smile did things to her insides that it really shouldn't be doing in a clinical situation—a work situation.

But Alex knew that what he'd said was true, not solely because of the medical procedure, but here she was in the hospital, with people she'd be working with for a long time to come—or so she hoped—and tiny seeds of friendship were being scattered around.

Will had disappeared but Alex waited with the nurse until Peter was fully awake.

The nurse wheeled in a smaller machine and attached new leads for an ECG to ensure the heart was stable while Alex spoke to her patient.

'I've had some drugs sent up from the pharmacy for you—I see you've been on them before—a blood thinner and a drug that slows the heart rate—instructions are on the boxes. You probably know the shock treatment could last a day, a week or six years, so I'd like you to stay on them for a month. See your own GP next week so he can check on you, then come and see me. Phone for an appointment in four weeks.'

Peter nodded, and thanked her, and she finally departed, leaving him eating cold hospital sandwiches and drinking a cup of tea.

'Want a cuppa yourself?' a nurse called as she came out.

'Yes, that sounds good,' Alex told her, as tiredness from what now seemed like another never-ending day swamped her.

Had it really only been this morning she'd driven into town to shop?

Had it only been three days since she'd arrived in Australia?

A cuppa was exactly what she needed, and she sank down onto the couch in a small tearoom behind the nurses' station and gratefully accepted one.

The woman who'd offered the tea had made herself a cup as well, and she settled herself on a chair opposite Alex.

'I remember you, you know,' she said. 'I was only a kid, but my family went to the same church and that bastard was always touching us kids. I feel ashamed now I didn't say something but at least my parents shifted us away from there. I remember Mum saying they treated you something cruel, those church people and your family.'

Alex shook her head, exhaustion hanging heavily in her body, but the woman's words had struck home.

'I hadn't even thought about people remembering,' she said. 'It was so long ago and so much must have happened since.'

Yet the woman on the phone had remembered…

'I don't think it'll bother you. I think these days people are far more aware of sexual abuse, and I bet a lot of the folk who thought him innocent changed their minds over time. You did right and I remember my mum saying how brave you were to stand up to him and all those others that reckoned he was God.'

Even in her tiredness, Alex found a smile.

'Thank you,' she said. 'That really makes me feel good, but right now I need to finish this cuppa and get home before I fall asleep. I start work in the morning, so I might pop in before I go to the rooms, if that's okay, and check on any patients I've got here.'

The nurse, whose name, belatedly, Alex read was Robyn, took her teacup, assured her she'd be welcome any time, and Alex found her way out of the hospital, across the road to the car park, then drove home very slowly, catching the last ferry and realising, as she spoke to the ferryman, that she'd have to find a bed somewhere in town for nights when she'd missed this last one. She wouldn't have liked to drive the long way round as tired as she was tonight.

And there'd be plenty of nights like this…

The chug of the ferry was soothing, and she drove off the ramp and along the river road.

It had been nearly twenty years but tonight it really felt as if she was coming home.

Until she saw the shattered window!

She couldn't help but notice it as she swung the car into the drive and the headlights shone straight onto the front of the house.

A bird, she decided, although coldness in her chest suggested that was wishful thinking.

Parking the car, she locked it and then the garage door, before walking along the front path, taking in the damage more closely.

The slope of the land, down towards the river, put this part of the house only a few feet above the ground, so by standing on tiptoe she could peer through the hole in the window and see the glass, glinting in the light from the streetlight outside, scattered over the floor and furniture in the living room.

She didn't see the rock until she went inside, or the note wrapped around it.

WHORE!

In blood-red letters!

She'd have to report it but right now she was just too tired, though finding a room in town was becoming a better and better idea.

Angry that the home she'd been so looking forward to had been rudely assaulted, she stomped through the rest of the place, checking there was no further damage.

Remembering Will coming in with the key from outside, she went back out and found the hollow rock, brought it and key inside.

Did people who made anonymous threats and threw rocks escalate to personal violence? She was sure she'd learnt something about these things in psychology lectures many years ago, but right now she couldn't think.

Glad she'd shopped, she checked the doors were locked, heated a ready meal in the microwave, ate most of it, and went straight up to her new bedroom.

Things would look better in the morning.

They didn't!

In fact, the broken window looked more menacing somehow.

She'd woken at six and after surveying the damage had phoned the police.

'I know you probably can't come out now,' she said, 'but I'm starting work and will be out all day and I want to get a glazier to fix the window as soon as possible.'

'Where do you work?' the policeman asked, and Alex explained.

'What if you could take a photo then put the rock and the note in a plastic bag and take them both to work? We'll send someone round to collect them and take a formal statement. Perhaps you could get your secretary or someone to phone and tell us a suitable time.'

Impressed by how obliging he was, Alex agreed, then she did an internet search and found a twenty-four-hour glass replacement firm. They could come in the early evening when she hoped she'd be home from work. It was the best she could do and, to her surprise, the positive actions she'd taken made her feel a whole lot better about the attack.

She fixed herself a simple fruit and cereal breakfast and took it out on the deck, sharing it with Buddy, who seemed to have forgotten about Bruce in his delight with being able to say, 'Such a wuss.'

'That could get old very quickly,' Alex told him—not that it made the slightest difference to his performance.

The nurse on duty in the coronary ward was as welcoming as Robyn had been the evening before. She found a space for Alex at the desk in the nurses' station so she could read the computerised records of the patients before she met them, then led Alex around the rooms, introducing the patients.

To her, they were a typical mix—a woman with congestive heart failure, a youngish man who'd just had a pacemaker implanted and should be discharged later in the day, another man undergoing tests, which would include an angiogram later that morning.

'Am I doing that?' Alex asked, as she hadn't seen any mention of it in the diary Marilyn had emailed to her.

'No, he's Mal Parker's patient and he'll do it today before he goes away. The doctors usually like to keep patients overnight before and after an angiogram.'

Alex nodded. If beds were available it was a wise move, as there could be complications after the procedure, including bleeding from the site through which the instruments had been threaded—in this case his groin—or reactions to the dye used to highlight problems.

'So I'll be discharging him tomorrow,' Alex said, and the nurse nodded.

'Unless he's asked Will Kent to see to it,' the nurse said. 'Will will be doing the anaesthetic,' she said, and Alex knew from the tingle in her nerve endings that Will was close.

'Mal has asked me to discharge him,' Will said cheerfully, 'so don't try to pinch my patients, Dr Hudson. You can have him back for his next appointment.'

Alex turned to face him.

He was in doctor gear—casual doctor gear, as befitted a hospital in a large coastal town. Under his unbuttoned white coat she could see a dark grey polo shirt and paler grey slacks.

With his stethoscope hanging out of his coat pocket and a wide grin in place, to Alex he was sex on legs.

Blimey! Was she *really* thinking things like that while she was at work?

'And good morning to you,' she said, hoping she sounded far cooler than she felt.

'Cardioversion was good, wasn't it?'

He sounded cool!

She nodded. It was easier than speaking, but she knew she had to get over this Will thing—and soon—because she was going to be seeing him around the hospital all the time.

But right now escape was the best option.

'I've got to fly. First patient due and you've already told me how fierce Marilyn can be if we run late.'

She whisked away, hoping it looked like professional haste, not a desperate escape bid.

Will watched her go, aware there was something bothering her.

Him?

Hardly!

'So, are you going to talk to your patient about his anaesthetic or just stand there, mooning over the pretty new doctor?' the nurse asked.

'I do not moon!' he said gruffly, although that probably *was* what he had been doing.

'She's really beautiful,' the nurse said in a kindly voice—perhaps excusing the mooning.

'I knew her way back when,' Will said firmly. 'She lived next door for a few years.'

'Oh, yeah,' the nurse teased as they went in together to see the patient. But he was also worried about the mooning. It was happening too fast, this attraction to Alex. And although he'd known her 'way back when', the attraction hadn't been there so he couldn't blame that for the way this had hit him.

He saw his patient, chatted to him about the upcoming operation and the light anaesthetic that he would be given, checked for allergies, discussed the weekend surf, and headed back to the ICU.

But the nurse's silly tease stayed with him, bringing this time a sense of foreboding.

He had Charlotte to consider, and an ill-conceived relationship could affect her, while an ill-fated one—which surely this would be—could be even more disastrous.

His ICU patients were all behaving themselves, more's the pity, because there wasn't an urgent problem to distract him from his thoughts.

Although there was always paperwork. He'd get on to that—letters to the general practice men and women whose patients he was tending.

He'd just have to try and keep images of Alex from flashing through his mind. Had he ever mooned over Elise? He'd loved her, he knew that, but early on in their relationship, had images of Elise flashed through his mind at inappropriate times?

The policeman came at five-thirty—Marilyn deciding it was too risky to try to schedule him between appointments. Her curiosity about the visit was evident but Alex was reluctant to explain, mumbling something about official stuff that had to be done and hoping Marilyn would assume it was to do with her father's death.

When he did come, a young constable, he was very sympathetic about the broken window, and he took the note and a copy of the photo but doubted it would be much help. Reluctantly, Alex told him of the phone call.

'But you've just arrived in town. Who could you possibly have upset?'

Alex shrugged. She looked into his pale blue eyes and realised, if he was a local, he could have been at kindergarten with the twins. The past would be unknown to him.

Did she have to tell him?

Not really, but now she'd reported it, and if the aggravation continued, wouldn't the police start looking for a reason?

Taking a deep breath, she said quietly, 'Before I left town more than fifteen years ago I upset a lot of people, including my parents. I can only think that there's someone out there who thinks I deliberately harmed them. I really, really do not want the whole situation stirred up again, but if this escalates then I suppose you'd have to look for someone from back then.'

The policeman looked puzzled and Alex regretted, more than anything, getting officials involved.

'I see,' he finally said, although it was obvious he didn't have a clue. 'We don't normally do patrols out on that side of the river, but I'm sure we can arrange for a car to drive that way from time to time. Maybe its presence might put a stop to this.'

Or not, Alex thought.

But the young man departed with her statement and the note, and finally she could go home—go home and get the window fixed.

Driving home wasn't quite the pleasure it had been the previous evening, but the trip across on the ferry soothed her, allowing her to slough off the tiredness of the day and feel renewed. It was dusk as she drew into the drive and as far as she could see there was no further damage.

Maybe it was over—whoever it was had got their anger off their chest and she'd been foolish bringing the police into it.

Maybe!

By Thursday she was certain the harassment had stopped. She'd settled in at work, was enjoying meeting her new patients, was getting to know the nurses at the hospital, and had been spared contact with Will, who was apparently in Sydney at a two-day seminar.

The patients behaved themselves so she was able to leave work early on Thursday, getting home in time to shower and change into casual clothes before Tony arrived.

She had a snack in case the meeting went for longer than her stomach could handle, and considered having a glass of wine to steel herself for the effort of her first social outing.

Best not, she'd decided.

Tony arrived on the dot of six.

'Were you waiting up the road until it was time?' she teased, and he smiled, and took her arm to lead her out to his robust four-wheel-drive, complete with not one but two kayaks on the top.

'Do you paddle one and lead the other, like people did with horses in the old days?'

He chuckled, a nice warm sound, and explained one was an old one a friend had given him, too small for him but he'd thought it might suit her.

'You're being very kind,' she said.

'Well, people were very kind to me when I first arrived in town. It's paying it forward, isn't it?'

So they chatted all the way to town, easy talk, very little of it personal, although they did establish that although he'd been married in the past, neither had children, and both were currently unattached.

It felt strange, getting back into the swing of social life. Strange to realise that this was the beginning of a friendship that could lead anywhere.

Perhaps not anywhere, Alex admitted to herself, given the spark of attraction was missing—at least on her part.

But friendship would be good. That's what she'd need as she settled back into her old home town.

And friendship she'd have, she decided later, if she joined the kayak club, for it was an extremely pleasant evening, listening to the club's plans for the next month, hearing the stories and feeling the camaraderie amongst the members, most of whom had gone on for a very noisy meal later.

'So, what do you think? Can you see yourself joining that crew?' Tony asked, as he drove her home after dinner.

'I can,' Alex admitted, for there'd been a warmth among the members and a feeling of welcome. 'But first I'll have to see if I can stay upright in a kayak.'

'I'm sure you'll manage,' Tony told her, 'and once you do you'll never give it up. Gliding silently through the backwaters of the river, or riding rapids, there's so much pleasure to be had.'

Alex could understand that, especially the silent gliding part for she usually switched off the tinnie's engine to glide among the mangroves.

They were nearly home and although Tony had shown

no indication he was interested in a more personal relationship, she did wonder if he'd try a kiss. And, ponder-
ing this, she was the last to see the desecration—the word
'Bitch' spray-painted in two-foot-high letters across the
front of her house.

'Good grief!' Tony growled. 'Who on earth would do
something like that?'

Alex felt sick, almost too sick to get out of the car.

'You can't stay here,' Tony said as she shrank against
the door. 'I've a spare bedroom. Let's get you whatever
you need and you can stay with me.'

It was a wonderful idea, and for a moment Alex was
tempted, then anger came to her rescue.

'No way,' she said, finding some of the fight that had
carried her through the court case all those years ago. 'I
will *not* let someone chase me out of my home.'

Especially not out of my beautiful new bedroom!

'Then I'll stay here,' Tony offered.

Suddenly exhausted, Alex shook her head.

'No, I'll be all right. I'm sure whoever did this is long
gone, and there are good locks on the doors, although
if you wouldn't mind just walking through the house
with me…'

The anger hadn't lasted long, that she'd made this pathetic plea to this man she barely knew.

He came, and together, turning on lights and checking each room, they walked through the house and out
onto the deck, where the moonlight turned the river to
a sheet of silver.

'I'm happy to stay,' he said, 'at least until the police
come. You *will* phone the police.'

'I'll ring them in the morning,' Alex promised.
'There's nothing can be done now.'

He gave her a hug, and when she walked him to the

door he dropped a swift kiss on her cheek—a kiss of comfort, nothing more.

A good friend in the making, she decided as she watched him drive away. But who was behind the harassment? Who could she possibly have hurt so much that nearly twenty years later they still held such bitter hatred towards her.

Saddened by this person's pain, and apprehensive now about her decision to return home, she took herself to bed, taking comfort from the river and from Buddy bouncing on her pillow.

'If only you could really talk, you could probably tell me who did this,' she told him, but all he did was ask who the pretty girl was.

At least that meant, worried as she was, that she drifted off to sleep with a smile on her lips.

CHAPTER SIX

THIS TIME THE noises outside her front door woke her—at the unearthly hour of five-thirty.

Fear gripped her for a moment, and then rational thought told her the harasser wouldn't be doing anything in broad daylight.

So who was doing what?

She walked through to her father's room and peered out the front window. Tony's big vehicle was pulled up on the kerb, and three, or maybe four, young men were scouring the front of her house with brooms and something that smelled like turpentine.

Tony was apparently supervising, and must have sensed her presence for he looked up and waved.

'I took plenty of photos for the police but thought you'd rather have it removed before the entire neighbourhood saw it. These lads are students of mine who think they might get extra credits for their good deed.'

'Well, I certainly hope they do,' Alex replied. 'Just give me ten minutes, I'll get some clothes on and organise coffee and toast for all of you. I think I might even have some croissants in the freezer.'

Tony smiled at her, and Alex felt a twinge of regret that the smile didn't provoke even a small tingle in her nerves.

It was a very nice smile, he was a very good-looking

man, he was kind and thoughtful and obviously clever—
his list of good attributes could probably go on for ever.

So why—?

She knew why, although she'd managed to put Will
out of her mind for the past few days.

Or almost out of her mind…

Tony and his crew finished their job and settled on
the deck, first helping her carry out all they would need
for their breakfast. They chatted easily, confident young
men, remarking on the beauty of the river, then moving
on to medical talk, telling her they'd probably see her
around the hospital before too long.

She thanked them for their help and was surprised
when, as they were leaving, one of them hung back.

'You know,' he said, 'we could easily make up a roster for someone to sleep out here with you until this is
sorted.'

The others jeered.

'In a spare bedroom or on your couch,' he growled.
'Just till they catch whoever did it.'

'Thank you,' Alex said, touched by their concern. 'But
Tony's already offered and I've assured him I'll be fine.'

More jeering and hooting but this time directed at
Tony. Would she, as a student, have treated the dean with
as much levity? Definitely not, but perhaps this was to
do with this being a smaller, more intimate university.
For whatever reason, it seemed healthier than the awe in
which she, as a student, had held the professors.

They departed, Tony telling her he'd left the kayak in
the shed beneath the house, beside the tinnie.

'And you should shift the key to the shed from above
the door—it's the first place a burglar looks.'

Alex laughed, but she would shift the key, and check
all the locks before she went to work. Tony would email

the photos to her to show the police and had even offered
to go to the police station with her, but she was feeling
stronger again, and ready now to fight this person or at
least find out who it was and why they felt she had ruined their life.

By lunchtime she was glad it was Friday, with two free
days ahead of her—well, free except for a ward round.

Getting back into the routine of work had taken more
out of her than she'd expected it would, so a relaxing
weekend—lazing on the deck with a good book, perhaps trying out the kayak—was looking very appealing.

Her phone line flashed.

Marilyn, to tell her Dr Kent wanted to see her after
her last patient at four.

'Thanks, Marilyn,' Alex responded, hopefully calmly,
although her heart was giving jittery little bumps. 'He's
probably picked up something that might interest me
from the seminar.'

Which made sense!

In fact, she hoped that was why he wanted to see her.

Or perhaps he just wanted to check out how her first
week had gone.

Another buzz on her phone told her the next patient
was waiting while she sat here thinking up excuses for
Will's visit so she wouldn't start thinking it was personal
and getting all excited!

You are thirty-six years old and should be over this
excited stuff, she told herself firmly. Besides, it would
never work.

She went out to meet her next patient.

But the Will who entered her office at four-thirty and
loomed over her desk certainly didn't look as if he'd come

for any social reason, neither, given the scowl on his face, did she think it was to pass on newly learned knowledge.

'Just what is going on in your life that I've had police questioning me about my actions?' he demanded, and Alex learned the meaning of dumbfounded.

'The police *what*?' she managed when she'd finally found her voice.

'Visited me at work, asking why my vehicle had been seen parked outside your house last night.'

His anger was hot enough for her to feel the sizzle of it across the desk. But when she'd made sense of what he'd said she found anger of her own.

'And what *was* your vehicle doing outside my house last night?'

He slumped into a chair.

'Foolish as it now seems, I got back from Sydney and thought I'd call in and see how your first week at work was going,' he muttered.

Not to see me—the thought breezed through her head, silly disappointment in its wake.

'I went out to a kayaking meeting—there's a group at the university—'

'I know all about the kayaking group at the uni—Tony Mitchell's lot.'

Uh-oh—so Will and Tony Mitchell didn't get on! That much was evident from the way he'd said the name.

'Ah, I get it!' Will continued, in a voice that could have frozen fire. 'He came to see you about your father—thought, gorgeous new woman in town, I must get to know her, and already you're in the kayaking group.'

'I am *not* in the kayaking group.' Alex spat the words at him. 'Yet!' she added, mostly out of spite. 'And Tony Mitchell asked me to the meeting as a kind gesture to a new person in town. I've only met him three times but he seems a thoroughly nice man and very helpful as well.'

'Three times?'

Alex sighed. She wasn't sure why but suddenly they were arguing about something that didn't really matter—except that it obviously did to Will.

Not that she had to explain anything to Will.

Of course she did—not only had he been incredibly kind since her arrival but he'd been there for her that last dreadful day in court.

'Tony brought some students around this morning to clean some offensive writing off the front of the house. I assume, as the police have spoken to you, you know about it.'

Will studied the weary-looking woman across the desk from him and wondered how the situation had developed into a heated argument.

Because he'd been shocked and concerned by the police visit?

Or because he was jealous of Alex's association with Tony Mitchell?

Deeply, gut-churningly jealous!

Which, given his ambivalence over the rights or wrongs of having a relationship other than friendship with Alex, was ridiculous.

He shrugged his shoulders and leaned across the desk to touch her hands, lightly clasped in front of her on the polished wood.

'I'm sorry, Alex. Charging in here and roaring at you. But when the police told me what had been happening, I couldn't believe you hadn't told me—talked to me about it.'

He saw shadows chase across her face but she didn't move her hands.

'At first it was just a phone call, and—you'd been so good, done so much already—I didn't want to seem a complete wimp by telling you about it. Then there was the rock and I did tell the police about that. It was only when Tony drove me home after the meeting and saw the writing on the wall that he became involved.'

She smiled, as if at some memory, and it took all Will's self-control not to tighten his grip on her hands at the mention of Tony Mitchell.

'Tony brought students out this morning to clean it up and they were so sweet, offering to set up a roster to sleep over each night so I wouldn't be alone.'

'I bet they did,' Will said, and Alex laughed.

'No, the young man who suggested it was very proper, offered to sleep on the couch. The others carried on but it was all good-natured and I know they'd have done it if I'd wanted it. I imagine to them I'm like an elderly aunt.'

'I doubt it,' Will said, 'but the boy was right, you shouldn't be in that house on your own.'

She moved her hands and stood up.

'Will, I haven't come home after all this time to that beautiful room my father made for me to be chased away by someone with a grudge.'

Will stood too, moving to the side of the desk, closer—wanting to touch her but still conflicted about it all.

'I can understand that,' he said gently, his anger forgotten in his concern for Alex. 'But if someone's nursed that grudge for twenty years, who knows what direction it might take next.'

She moved now, closing the distance between them, putting her hand on his arm and looking up into his face.

'I know, it worries me too, but I *won't* be hounded out of my home.'

How could he not kiss her?

He was thinking of a cheek kiss but somehow her lips were right there, and once his mouth had touched them he was lost, especially as she was making breathy little sounds that seemed to indicate she didn't mind the kiss at all.

Soft, pliant lips, tasting new and fresh, tasting of the river, and sunlight, and beginnings and maybe endings...

His mind buzzed with sensations he couldn't possibly be feeling, yet kissing Alex was like nothing else he'd ever done before. Kissing Alex was a journey and a revelation, and he gathered her closer, nestled her in his arms, fingers wanting to explore, but his mind insisting he concentrate—for now—on the kiss...

Alex knew her bones were melting. Bone-melt from a kiss was something she'd heard of but had never experienced so right now, given she had Will to lean on, she was going to explore it fully.

His skin was just a little rough—as if he hadn't shaved since early morning—but the roughness, when it caught her skin, was tantalising in some way.

His lips demanded and she gave, his tongue invaded, and she welcomed it, tasting, testing, right where she'd wanted to be since first meeting Will again, for all she still felt, deep down somewhere she couldn't find right now, that it couldn't work.

She'd failed other relationships but to get into one where there was a young vulnerable child and fail that?

Unthinkable!

She was easing away from his body when an angry buzzing from the desk broke them fully apart, and, seeing the time, Alex realised Marilyn must still be in the outer room, perhaps waiting for Alex to leave so she could lock up.

And here she'd been kissing Will with such abandon when anyone could have walked in!

Alex pressed the key and spoke to her office manager.

'I'll lock up,' she said to the unseen Marilyn. 'Will's got some stuff to pass on from the seminar, so you go on home.'

Would Marilyn go without poking her head in to say goodbye? Alex hoped not because she knew her lips would be swollen, her cheeks reddened from the kiss, and her clothes probably not as neat as they might be.

'Just don't forget to lock the inner doors as well,' Marilyn reminded her, before adding, 'Goodnight, Dr Kent,' in a voice that suggested she knew full well why the pair of them had forgotten the time.

Alex looked at the man she'd been kissing.

'I don't know, Will,' she said, sighing wearily to underline the futility of the words. 'I'm afraid to get into a relationship with you—afraid I'd let you down.'

'I doubt you could ever do that,' he said, yet she heard a shadow of doubt in his words.

Unfortunately, he smiled and spoiled all the determination she'd been mustering.

'But I do know I'm hungry,' he announced, 'and no matter what rubbish we've got in our heads about this attraction between us, we do still have to eat.'

'Fish and chips on my deck?'

Alex regretted the words before they were fully out of her mouth.

Will grinned.

'Or fish and chips at the beach, so you could look at the ocean for a change, but perhaps, until we're a bit surer about where this is going—how we feel about a relationship between us—I think we should stick to restaurants. There's a great Indonesian place in town, or Greek, if you fancy throwing plates.'

'Indonesian,' Alex said. 'I feel like spicy but not too hot.'

'Do you now?' he whispered, and kissed her again, but briefly this time, finishing the kiss with a brush of his fingers down her cheek.

'I'd have said very hot,' he teased, and she knew she'd reacted with a blush.

Alex waited until they'd ordered and were sipping a pleasant fruit cocktail before she asked the question that had been burning in her brain.

'Why aren't *you* sure where this is going or how you feel about a relationship between us?'

He took her hand. 'Are you?'

She shook her head but persisted. 'No, but don't answer a question with a question. Why?'

He smiled and the way his eyes crinkled at the corners almost halted her breathing.

They're wrinkles, for heaven's sake, a voice in her head scolded, but she'd already moved on to study his lips as he spoke, and the way he ran his fingers through his hair when he was...

Frustrated?

Well, so was she but he *was* trying to explain so at least she should listen.

She was a woman, she could do two things at once, so look and listen.

But, even listening, he didn't seem to be making much sense.

'Excuse me,' she said, aware she should have been lis-

tening more closely, 'but are you saying the attraction is
nothing more than frustration because neither of us has
been in a relationship for a while?'

He gave a huff of laughter that suggested more despair than humour.

'That's what I don't know. It's just I've never felt like
this before—never experienced almost instant attraction,
not with Elise, not with any woman—so I have to think
it must just be frustration.'

Hand in the hair again, long, slim fingers—clever fingers—

'Then there's love!' He blurted out the word as if it
was anathema to him. 'What if we get into a relationship and it leads to love? And then there's Charlotte…'

He took her hands and squeezed her fingers. 'See,
I'm a mess.'

Ah, that made sense—the falling in love thing, not
the mess. He'd lost the woman he'd loved—been so hurt
by it he didn't want to risk it ever again. She wanted to
get up and go around and hug him, tell him it was okay.

Not that her own situation was much better.

'I agree with you about Charlotte,' she said, hoping to
get his mind off lost love. 'Not that I don't love children
but the fact I haven't been able to make a relationship
work before worries me. I don't want to get involved with
you to the extent I get to know her, too, then it all falls
apart. I don't think that would be fair to her.'

'So you're a mess as well,' Will said, almost cheerfully, 'and the whole thing's a mess and perhaps it's better if we just hope it all goes away.'

'Do you think it will?' Alex asked him, and when he
smiled this time, she knew the answer, at least from her
side of things.

The shake of Will's head confirmed his thoughts and

fortunately their meal arrived or they'd probably have kissed again, right there in the restaurant, then left without eating if the urgency Alex was feeling was any guide.

'Saved by the rijsttafel,' Will joked.

'And *my* gado gado!'

They shared the meals, and ate, and talked of Alex's first week at work, and the seminar Will had attended in Sydney, but the thread of desire had thickened to a rope and it tightened between them until words became impossible.

'I'll follow you home,' Will said as they left the restaurant, and although Alex protested, she knew she'd feel safer if he was there....

But the reminder of the harassment broke the spell between them and she realised she couldn't go on needing the support of someone every time she drove home after dark.

'How did the police get on to you?' she asked, as he held the car door open for her.

'Apparently they questioned everyone in the street, and a neighbour had seen my car. I stopped it and phoned you because the house was in darkness.'

'Was it late?'

'Eightish, I suppose,' he said, bending down so he could hold her hand as he spoke. 'I guess the neighbours went to bed before the real culprit turned up with the paint. Look, are you sure you won't stay with me—well, not me but with Mum? Or get a hotel room in town?'

Alex reached up so she could kiss his cheek.

'While we're both so confused?' she teased. 'You know full well we'd end up in bed in that hotel room, and right now I think that would make things worse instead of better. Besides, there's Buddy, and I really love my house, Will, and I *won't* be hounded out of it.'

* * *

The courage of her statement shook him. She was something special, this woman...

But hadn't they just agreed the attraction between them couldn't go anywhere?

His churning thoughts made it impossible to speak so he nodded, kissed her cheek, shut the door and went to his own car. At least she hadn't protested about him following her home.

He pulled into the drive behind her and waited while she came out, lowering the garage door with the remote.

'No graffiti tonight,' she said, but a quaver in her voice suggested she wasn't feeling nearly as brave as she made out.

He grew angry again that someone had targeted her like this—as if she hadn't been through enough—and the dark outline of a car parked on the verge about four houses up disturbed him as well. He'd check it out before he went home.

'You're looking at that car up there,' Alex said, and Will remembered just how observant she was. 'It's probably a neighbour's visitor, or one of my student fans taking on the job of guardian.'

'I'll check it anyway,' Will promised, although now he thought he recognised the shape of it—a shape very like the big four-wheel-drive Tony Mitchell drove.

He took her key and opened the door for her, ducked as Buddy swooped out the door then back in again to land on Alex's shoulder.

'He doesn't seem upset,' Alex said, but Will was more concerned about the futility of having a bird as one's only protection.

'You should get a dog,' he told Alex, who laughed.

'And leave the poor thing on its own all day? I'd have

to get a dog-walker and a vet and Buddy mightn't take to him and then where would I be?'

'Safer, if it was a big dog,' Will growled, but he knew it was a losing battle and changed tack—thinking of the weekend ahead of them.

'Can I see you tomorrow?' he asked. 'I'm on call again so Mum's taken Charlotte up the coast to my sister's place. She has three little ones and Charlotte adores them. We could have an early surf, the tide would be in, and the waves are forecast to be small but curlers. Then we could finish with breakfast at the surf club.'

'You and Dave were always surfing. You still surf?'

Will met her eyes.

'It's the one thing that kept me sane after Elise died,' he said, and Alex understood.

How often, way back then, had she taken the children to the beach to explore the rock pools while Dave and Will had surfed and Isobel had sat on the veranda of the surf club, reading, until it had been time for them to join her for breakfast.

Thinking back to that time, she realised that playing with the children and their innocent, non-judgemental love for her had been a huge part of her recovery from the trauma and torment of that time. As surfing had obviously been for Will...

Lecca, the twins had called her, and rarely had ten minutes gone by without one or other of them, often both, flinging themselves into her arms for a hug.

'Lecca, we love you,' they would say, and slowly their love had made her whole again.

Could she revisit that time again?

With another child?

Not yet!

Not until she was really sure she could handle a relationship—not make a botch of it, ruin it, possibly hurt the child...

But she *could* go to the beach! *Could* explore the rock pools and remember more good things of the past.

'I'd love it. I'll meet you there. What time?'

CHAPTER SEVEN

MEETING HIM THERE meant he wouldn't have to drive her home, come back into the house and thus put them together in close proximity of a bed. Will saw that immediately and supposed it was wise.

Not that he felt very wise, mostly frustrated, not sexually frustrated—well, that too—but frustrated that his usually intelligent brain couldn't seem to work out how to handle his attraction to Alex.

'Six-thirty too early? You'll surf?'

She laughed.

'Will, don't you remember when you and Dave tried to teach me to surf? Didn't I tell you then that the river was my watery habitat, like the surf was yours? But I love the rock pools, the sea anemones and little, brilliantly coloured crabs. I'll be very happy there while you brave the waves.'

He smiled and pulled her close, intending just a brief, goodbye kiss, but she kind of melted against him and he was lost, claiming her mouth again, seeking to know her through the touch of lips and tongue.

They were both flushed—he could feel the heat in his cheeks—and breathless when she eased away from him.

'Doesn't seem to be going away, this attraction, does

it?' she said, trying for casual, but her voice too huskily intense to carry it off.

'We'll work it out,' he assured her, pulling her back to where he was beginning to feel she belonged—right there in his arms.

She nestled there and he held her, breathing in a faint lemon scent from her shampoo, and woman smell, the scent of Alex.

Once again it was she who broke the embrace.

'Six-thirty in the morning,' she said, and kissed him lightly on the cheek.

She stood in the doorway as he left, and he couldn't help glancing up the road, pleased to see the big four-wheel-drive had departed.

Although now he remembered what had brought him to follow Alex home this evening, he began to wonder if perhaps she did need someone to keep an eye on her—or at least her house—overnight. She'd waved as he'd got into his car, then disappeared inside, shutting the door behind her. He knew she'd lock it, but the thought of someone attacking her house while she was in it made him feel extremely uneasy.

Feeling foolish, he turned his car and drove up the road, as if he was driving away, then turned around and passed the house again, now only lit on the river side—Alex had obviously gone up to her bedroom. He parked where the man he'd thought might be Tony had been parked, and sat for a while, contemplating what he knew was foolishness.

The buzz of his pager stopped further speculation, and lights going on at the front of Alex's house suggested she, too, had received a message.

Rather than use his mobile he returned to Alex's house and knocked on the door. He could hear her voice so she must be just inside. The door opened, the phone still in her hand. Not wanting to interrupt her call, he listened as she spoke, although the words '…if you get an anaesthetist there to do a TOE. I'm on my way' weren't very revealing.

Finishing the phone conversation, she turned to him.

'Patient I haven't seen yet, Paul Wilcox, fifty-nine, apparently phoned the ambulance with ripping, tearing pains in his chest, going through to his back. He's one of Mal's patients and I glanced through his file—suffers from hypertension and Mal suspected an aortic aneurysm but the bloke hadn't got around to having the tests Mal ordered—or he's had them and there were no results in the file. Ambos report shortness of breath, sweating, weaker pulse in one side and some paralysis. They gave him morphine for the pain and beta blockers to slow his heart rate, and he's due at the hospital about now.'

'I'll drive,' Will said. 'If there was an aneurysm and it's ruptured, he'll have bled out before we get there.'

It sounded harsh but the empathy in Will's voice told Alex he was simply stating an unnerving fact.

'Or it's an aortic dissection and, depending where it is, we'll need someone to operate,' Alex guessed. 'You were paged?'

She knew it was an unnecessary question, but she was trying to switch fully to medical mode, something that used to be so easy back when Will hadn't been around.

Will nodded, but he was either concentrating on getting them to the hospital in the shortest possible time or he, too, was switching to his medical persona.

'What will you do?' he asked.

'They'll do a CT scan as soon as the ambulance unloads him. If something shows up on the scan—a problem in the ascending aorta—we'll do a TOE when we get there to get a clearer picture of just where it is and how bad it is, always given the first scan shows dissection. I've asked for an anaesthetist to be on standby for the TOE—oh, I suppose that's why they paged you.'

'The transoesophageal echocardiogram, that magic invention,' Will said. 'You know the Americans call it a TEE, like the thing you put under a golf ball, because they spell oesophagus with an "e". I'm always amazed how close we can get the probe to the heart.'

It was conversation, and Alex, focussed on her patient, didn't reply, too busy wondering just what facilities the hospital had and how easy or otherwise it would be for them to operate on the patient tonight.

They'd paged Will, so presumably—

She *had* to ask!

'If it's a type-A dissection in the ascending aorta, is the hospital equipped for an emergency op? For cardio-pulmonary bypass? Do they have a cardiovascular surgical team? Would they have a synthetic graft, say, to help with the repairs? Could they rally enough people in to manage the whole complex procedure?'

Will didn't answer immediately, too busy driving carefully onto the ferry, but once he'd switched off the engine he turned to her.

'Hey, they didn't open a cardiovascular surgical unit to play around with angiograms and cardioversions that even docs like you can do,' he teased. 'We've got the lot and an absolutely fantastic staff who all know they are permanently on call—mainly because of the young lad who needs the new heart. It's a regional centre of excellence, so the hospitals in nearby coastal and inland towns send their patients here.'

'Patients who would previously have gone to Sydney,'

Alex mused, still considering the complexity of the operation that might lie ahead for Mr Wilcox.

She could understand Will's pride in the service the hospital offered when they arrived to see the efficient machine already gathering pace. The patient was in Theatre, the CT scan up on a screen, a radiologist ready to do the TOE, which, once done, clearly showed where the aorta had formed into two channels.

Will introduced her to Norm Wright, the cardiovascular surgeon.

'You'll assist?' Norm asked, before heading off to change and scrub.

'Love to,' Alex assured him.

'And, Will, you'll play number two to the anaesthetist?'

'When don't I?' grumbled Will, then he turned and smiled at Alex. 'The hospital board's been advertising for a new anaesthetist, and, though we've a couple of trainees, for jobs like this they hook me in.'

He smiled as he finished the explanation and Alex's heart skipped a beat.

You can't go into Theatre with heart skips, she told herself firmly, and by the time she was gowned, masked and scrubbed, she actually believed it.

The team was just as efficient as Will had said it would be. Once in Theatre, he introduced her to the perfusionist, who would run the heart-lung machine, monitor the patient's blood, and administer the drug to stop the heart while the actual operation took place.

The anaesthetist, a woman, was at the head of the table, Will beside her, their eyes already trained on the monitor, trays of equipment were in place, and the assisting doctors and nurses were talking quietly as they waited for orders.

A younger surgeon opened the patient's chest, Alex falling easily into place in the team, responding to requests to cauterise small vessels, twisting clamps to hold the chest open.

The perfusionist worked neatly and swiftly to connect the patient to the bypass machine, and on Norm's nodded command injected the cardioplaegic solution that slowed down the heart to near stopping but kept it alive with rich nutrients.

The bulge where the dissection had taken place was clearly visible, but Norm checked all around it, making sure no other vessels were affected. Alex watched the way his gloved fingers moved, so deftly, so surely, and listened as he talked the team around him through the whole procedure.

With the tear repaired, Norm slipped a polyester sleeve around the damaged part of the big blood vessel, checked there was no more obvious damage anywhere, and nodded to the perfusionist to stop the cardioplaegia. It was always a 'hold the breath' moment. If the heart didn't start on its own, it would need a shock to get it going, but, to everyone's relief, it began a steady beat.

Next step in the procedure was to check for blood leaking from the damaged artery, but the repair was secure and the job of closing the patient's chest began.

Norm left the theatre as his assistant was closing, and the anaesthetist handed the patient over to Will.

Alex, too, stayed, assisting with the closure, waiting until the patient, accompanied by Will, was wheeled into Recovery.

Knowing he would stay there until the patient regained consciousness, Alex made her way to the locker rooms, where she showered and changed back into civilian clothes.

Felt in the pockets of her slacks for her car keys then remembered she'd driven in with Will.

She poked her head into the recovery room, and was surprised to see Will handing over to a younger man.

'Saved by the wonderful Dr Turner,' Will said. 'A very virtuous young intensivist who's early for his shift.'

Relief and tiredness mingled in his smile, and Alex was surprised to see it was after five o'clock. It had been late when they'd started, probably close to midnight, so it had been a five-hour op—tiring for anyone.

'You're *not* tired?' he demanded, apparently disconcerted that she was still on her feet.

She smiled at him. 'I will be now I know how long I've been standing up in there,' she told him. 'What next? Do you stay?'

He shook his head. 'No, it's over to Dr Turner now. I'll look in on him again before I leave the hospital, and then he'll be my patient once he's in the ICU, but I wouldn't think they'll move him there for some hours yet.'

Another smile, this one a better effort.

'Breakfast at the surf club?'

'They wouldn't be open,' Alex protested, although the mention of breakfast had made her realise she was hungry and if she wanted to sleep she'd need to eat first.

'They will by the time I've showered and dressed again,' Will said, standing up and touching her lightly on the arm. 'Do you mind waiting?'

She shook her head, even so light a touch rendering her momentarily mute.

'So I'll see you down at the car in half an hour, okay?'

Was it the smile or the light touch on her arm that had ignited her nerves again?

Or just plain tiredness?

Alex sighed. She knew it wasn't tiredness...

But was it love?

How could she tell?

She'd thought she'd been in love when she'd got engaged. It had only been later she'd realised that love hadn't really come into it. A certain amount of attraction, for sure, and liking, and friendship, and all kinds of good things, but love?

Love felt like a foreign country and right now, if what she was feeling for Will was love, it was a very confusing country where she knew neither the language nor the customs.

CHAPTER EIGHT

THE SUN WAS coming up over the ocean, colouring the world with a golden sheen. The low waves Will had forecast curled onto the beach in a froth of whiteness then receded, leaving shining wet sand behind. A few surfers were out on boards, but for once Will didn't envy them. Sitting here with Alex had filled him with a sense of peace he hadn't felt for a long time.

The operation had gone well, which added to his feeling of well-being, but it was the woman opposite him, the sun glinting off the gold of her hair, her blue eyes shining as she took in the scene and breathed in the air, that made him feel...complete?

It was okay! It would work. He'd *make* it work.

'You look very serious.'

Her teasing smile filled him with warmth the sun itself couldn't match.

'Very,' he said, with an answering smile. 'I was deciding that we've got to stop dithering about the past and look to the future—see where whatever it is between us takes us, with no hang-ups, no doubts, no looking back.'

She reached out and took his hand, her face aglow with what he'd like to think was love but which was probably just the morning sunlight.

'Yes, let's,' she said, and, for the moment, that was

enough, until she added, 'But cautiously—there's Charlotte, remember, and she shouldn't be hurt.'

A shadow crossed his contentment because he knew Alex was right. If they got too close and things didn't work out, his daughter *would* be hurt. It was a thought not very far from his mind at all times.

But that was for tomorrow—for now, surely, they could explore today!

He tackled the breakfast the waitress had placed in front of him—the surf club's renowned 'big' breakfast.

'Can you eat all that?' Alex asked, looking up from her tasty-looking scrambled eggs.

'Just watch me,' Will challenged. He began on the sausages—small sausages—pushing Alex's fork away when she sneaked it over to pinch a slice, although he did—later—drop a slice on her plate.

Silly stuff, but the tension, not only of the operation but of the last, well, four years really drained out of him and he relaxed, listening to Alex talk about her work in Glasgow—where the sun never came up over the ocean for breakfast—and telling her a little of his own life since he'd moved back to Heritage Port.

Getting-to-know-you stuff, but here, on his favourite beach at sunrise, it took on a special significance, as did the woman with whom he was sharing the experience.

Will was in an odd mood, Alex decided, but obviously a happy one. Every now and then he smiled for no apparent reason. She sneaked glances at him as he ate—almost total concentration on his breakfast at first—and it seemed as if the faint lines in his face had smoothed out, and a tension she'd sensed since first meeting him again had eased from his body.

Because he'd put the past behind him?

Because he was coming to the end of his grieving?

Hadn't he said something? Something about how surfing had helped him heal after his wife had died?

But he'd also said he was afraid of love…

Could anything less than love work?

And what did *she* know of love?

Vague uneasiness stirred inside her, but she pushed it aside, ate her eggs, and decided Will was right—she would look to the future.

Just because her past relationships had failed, it didn't mean…

He looked up and caught her watching him. He smiled and blew a kiss, and this time the stirring was completely different, and, tired as she was after a night without sleep, she began to hope he'd stay when he'd driven her home.

Although—

'I came back to town with you but I can get a cab home,' she told him. 'That way we can both have a sleep and maybe get together later.'

'Or better yet, we both go to my place for a sleep and I'll drive you home later?'

The roguish gleam in his eyes told her exactly how much sleep he expected they'd have.

'We go to your place for a *sleep*?' she repeated, and he laughed and squeezed her hand.

'We could have a sleep later,' he suggested, but whether it was tiredness or the doubts that had sneaked in about grieving and love Alex suddenly felt it was all going too fast.

'Much more sensible that I get a cab home and see you later,' she said firmly, although she softened the words with a smile and a return squeeze of his fingers.

'Do we want sensible?' he grouched, and now she saw the tiredness in his face.

'Today we do,' she said. 'Well, for this morning at least! We're both too tired for much else.'

'It's age, isn't it?' he grumbled, but Alex knew he'd agreed. 'But no cabs,' he added. 'I'll drive you home. It's only another half-hour there and back.'

They left the surf club hand in hand, and she rested her fingers on his thigh as he drove her home.

'Just drop me off, no need to get out,' she said, as he opened his door.

'No?' he said, climbing out of the car and reminding her of the problems she'd had during the week.

'Is that why you insisted on driving me home?' she asked, as they walked together to the front door, but Will didn't answer, turning her instead and attempting to walk her, none too gently, back towards his vehicle.

But Alex glanced over her shoulder and saw the tiny pink and grey bundle outside the door.

'Buddy!' she cried, breaking away from Will and racing forward.

The galah was definitely dead, but as Alex lifted the bird's stiff body she heard the raucous cry from inside.

'It's not Buddy,' she said, thrusting the bird at Will so she could open the door. 'It's just a stuffed bird. A piece of taxidermy.'

She opened the door and the grey and pink bullet sped towards her, landing on her shoulder and scolding her loudly for being out all night.

Tears of relief she couldn't hold back were running down her cheeks, and Buddy, sensing her distress, brushed his head against them, quieter now, but still scolding his 'pretty girl'.

'That settles it,' Will said, passing her in the hall and heading for the kitchen. 'I'm staying while you sleep, then you can pack a bag and come to my place—stay in

Mum's flat. I'll put the bird into a bag and take it into the police station this afternoon.'

With Buddy still on her shoulder, Alex sank down into a lounge chair.

'Who could hate me so much?' she whispered, when Will returned.

Will had no answer except to ease her out of the chair and take her in his arms, holding her close until the tears were spent, then guiding her feet upstairs to the big bedroom with its view out to the river she loved.

Later, when they'd both caught up on some sleep, they'd have to talk—to go back to the time they'd first met and try to work out who she might have upset so much that the anger still burned.

'I upset everyone I knew,' she murmured, as if she was following his thoughts, but when he began to ease the tunic she'd been wearing off over her head she didn't protest, simply helped him, then pulled off her leggings herself.

'Let's just go to bed,' she said, and Will knew it wasn't an invitation to do any more than be together—to share the bed—and hopefully sleep, although now his mind was churning with ways and means to track down whoever was tormenting Alex.

Preferably before the attacks escalated to violence against Alex herself…

Alex turned in her sleep, or half turned as she met a warm body. Memories of the long night, breakfast at the beach then returning home.

Will…

He must have stirred for now his arm came around her, drawing her close, so she was spooned against his body, and, secure in his arms—secure in a way she hadn't felt for so long—she slept again.

Until, slowly, an awareness grew—awareness of his body, of his body's reaction to hers—and still half-asleep she moved so the arm that held her close shifted and his hand rested on her breast, caressed it gently—awakening *her* body as his was awakening.

'You're still asleep,' Will murmured, his lips warm against her shoulder. 'Bad time to make decisions.'

But his hand had left her breast and was trailing across her stomach. Her nerves were alert to every touch while her body ached for more.

Ached for more?

When had her body ever ached for anything, let alone more?

She must have stiffened for his hand stilled, lay flat on her stomach, warm and kind of heavy.

And the breasts he'd touched felt heavy too—sensitised and...

His lips pressed against her shoulder, against the base of her neck—surely that couldn't be an erogenous zone—but now they'd slid to kiss the sensitive hollow below her ear, firing such erotic responses she felt breathless.

Certain she'd end up pulling away, disappointing him, she turned and traced her fingers across his face, kissed his lips then drew back to look at him.

Or could it work?

Sleepy brown eyes, unshaven chin, lips that asked to be kissed.

She kissed them again and sighed.

Looked into those now serious brown eyes.

'This is where things usually break down in my relationships,' she whispered, touching his face again, tracing the laugh lines near his eyes. 'I *have* tried before,

but I go all stiff and cold and somehow the few men I've
known found that off-putting.'

'But you've never tried with Superman!' he teased,
and she smiled and let him draw her close, let him wrap
his arms around her and hold her against his warm body.

'If this is all you want, Alex, that's okay. Just lie there,
let me hold you, let's just be together in a nice warm bed
while the rest of the world goes by.'

She snuggled closer, confused now, the ache for more
still there. Will's hands caressed her back, her neck, fingers kneading her scalp, and she moved her hands against
his back, feeling the muscles over the bone, then higher,
feeling the shape of his head, the tension in his neck...

'It isn't really okay, is it,' she said, as she, in turn,
kneaded, but his neck muscles, not his scalp.

He drew back so this time he could look at her, and
the hint of laughter was back in his eyes.

'We'll work it out,' he promised. 'I can understand
physical intimacy being hard for you, but it's not a walk in
the park for me either, and this instant attraction thing—
well, that's just plain scary.'

'Superman scared?'

'Very,' he said, serious again, although when he kissed
her it didn't feel like a scared kiss.

Maybe a little tentative, but only until she kissed him
back, opened her mouth to his tongue, and pressed close
to his body again.

How long they kissed for she had no idea, but when
Will eased away, sat up in bed and announced that was
enough for one day, she felt devastated.

Or her body felt devastated...

He *had* to go!

He had to go right now, or things would escalate and

he'd lose this woman altogether, and although he couldn't really understand it, he knew he couldn't let that happen.

Will was trying to untangle himself not only from Alex but from the sheets yet still retain enough covering to hide his burgeoning erection.

Her hand touched his hip.

'Stay?'

Nothing more than a sibilant whisper but it tightened his groin even more.

Now Alex was sitting up, sitting behind him, her arms around his chest, her fingers brushing against his nipples in such a way he almost groaned with agony.

'Help me?'

The words were pressed against his shoulder and, given his condition, there was no way he should have agreed.

But somehow they were lying down again, well, Alex lying down, he resting his head on his elbow, lying on his side so his reaction would be less obvious.

He looked into the beseeching blue eyes and knew he was lost.

'Are you sure?' he asked.

She nodded then reached up to trace his lips with a fingertip.

'Just show me how, Superman, show me how it could be,' she whispered.

Will took a long, deep breath. A cold shower would have been better but hardly appropriate at this time.

'So, first we kiss,' he said, determined not to rush her, wanting desperately to show her how enjoyable consensual sex could be. 'But while we kiss we can explore each other—that's what hands are for. Are you okay with that?'

She nodded again but this time he detected the hint of a smile on her so-delectable lips.

So, lying side by side, they kissed, and while his hands stroked and teased her back and breasts and belly, hers, more tentative, sent fire flashing through his body.

He slipped his mouth away from hers, kissing her ear, nibbling at the lobe, kissed his way down her neck while she pressed kisses against his head.

She stiffened when his mouth closed very gently around a nipple, but before he could pull away she'd relaxed and her hands were holding his head to her breasts.

Urgent sensations speared from Alex's breast to her sensitive core, and her body shuddered with something she supposed must be desire. Will's attentions to her breast immediately stopped and she had to hold his head to show she wanted more.

Well, she thought she wanted more…

And now it all became a little confusing, sensations she'd never known swamping her body and anaesthetising her brain.

Will's teeth were teasing at her nipples, first one then the other, while his hand was sliding down her body, finger tickling at her navel, hand sliding lower, fingers gently brushing against the lips, touching and retreating, each retreat a tease that notched her tension higher.

She was mindless now, beyond thought, giving in to the sensual eroticism of Will's touch, so when his fingers slid into her she shuddered, but it was a shudder of a different kind. And now those clever fingers were touching her inside and out, moving slowly then swiftly, then slowing again—teasing. She knew he was teasing because the tension building inside her was close to an eruption of some kind, but not, she knew, even in her dazed state, a frightening eruption.

So when it came, the explosive release, she thrashed

on the bed, shuddering again, pins and needles racing from her toes up to her scalp, her body so light only Will's arms anchored her to earth.

She snuggled against him, spent but confused, aware this was a two-way thing and now it would—or should—be her turn to pleasure Will.

But Will seemed unfazed, his hand, still now, between her legs, his other arm holding her close.

As sense returned, with it came sensation and she knew she wanted more—possibly needed more.

So it was up to her.

She slid back enough to run her hands across his chest, and kissed him as her thumbs brushed his nipples. Kept kissing him, feeling his response, not only in the kiss but in the tightening of his body.

'Be very sure,' he whispered against her lips, and as she swallowed the breath of the words she felt for him, guiding him into her wetness, letting him fill her as tremors from her orgasm still lingered.

Moving with him now, feeling his body heavy on hers, feeling *his* desire rising in the urgency of his movements, her own building again until an even stronger release matched his, her cry echoing in his groan.

They lay, still joined, entwined, replete for now, the sun on the river throwing shadows on the ceiling, then Will slid to one side and leaned again on his elbow, looking down at her.

'Okay?' he asked huskily.

'Very okay,' she replied, then smiled at him. 'Maybe you really are Superman.'

He was about to protest but she stilled him with a finger to his lips.

'I need to talk,' she said, 'to tell you—to explain.'

He nodded, but wrapped his arm around her so she was close as she poured out all the pain and hurt of her old relationships—all two of them.

'I'm not an idiot, Will, I knew I needed help. I went to psychologists, counsellors, even, one time in Glasgow, to a sex clinic. I learnt how to give myself an orgasm, but it seemed an empty and not particularly pleasurable exercise so when that didn't help I decided to forget about both sex and intimate relationships. Plenty of people live without both, why couldn't I?'

Will had to smile. 'Perhaps because you're a beautiful, vibrant, sensual woman, and deep down you knew it wasn't enough?'

She gave a light laugh that had more than a touch of cynicism in it, and he knew immediately that the shadows of her past still hung darkly over her life.

Life!

What was he doing, lolling around in bed with her, when right now the priority had to be keeping her safe?

'I could stay here like this for ever,' the woman he was worrying about murmured, eyes slumberous again, body stretching lazily.

Temptingly!

His response was to tighten his arms around her, but only for a moment.

'Tempting though it is, my love,' he answered, 'there's stuff to do. Shall we save water and shower together?'

Alex's mind spun—he'd called her his love—stuff to do, like dead birds—and showering together, being naked together. Hadn't they skipped a big part of the getting-to-know-you thing?

Uncertainty gripped her, the 'my love' endearment forgotten as all the early awkwardness of an intimate relationship hit home. It had been so long since she'd been this close to anyone, and never really successfully.

Part of the prudery her fiancé had accused her of, she knew, but now?

With Will?

'I'll start the shower,' he said, as if sensing her confusion, 'and then I'm going to come back and take you by the hand and lead you in there, where I'm going to soap you all over and sluice it off you and not do one thing you would not like me doing, okay?'

But before he could put his words into actions she turned towards him and put her arms around him, burying her face in his shoulder.

'I might not be very good at all this.'

She blurted out the words, wanting them said, willing him to understand, but feeling incredibly foolish and naïve.

His arms locked around her.

'You are a beautiful, sexy, glorious woman who has been treated very badly in the past, not only by that rat Spencer but, I suspect, also by other men in your life. But your body's response to mine was unbelievable so do not, ever, doubt your sexuality.'

He kissed her lips, a long, seductive kiss that had the nerves she'd never felt before responding once again.

'We don't have to shower together,' he said, when he finally moved his lips from hers. 'In fact, I'll shower very quickly and go pick up dinner because we need to eat, while you can have the shower all to yourself and think about the times we *will* share it, okay?'

His eyes were wary, as if he feared he'd upset her in some way, so this time *she* kissed *him*, whispering as she drew back, 'So much more than okay,' although all kinds of doubts still lingered in her head.

She showered quickly herself, phoned the hospital—patient doing well—then made a salad to go with whatever he brought back from the co-op, keeping busy to keep her mind off what had happened, although that was impossible because her body had such vivid recollections of it that just remembering made her want to be back in Will's arms again.

Was this lust?

She had no idea, although she now knew, in her body as well as in her head, that sex was meant to be enjoyed, and, even more importantly, that she had the ability to enjoy it.

Had it happened too quickly?

The question nagged at Will as he drove to the co-op, but the pleasure that still lingered in his body told him the answer was a definite no.

Alex's response to his foreplay had been so volcanic it had electrified his own desire, and even thinking about it now made him hard.

But he guessed she'd never experienced a shared orgasm before and the intensity of it had shaken her, and had probably brought back all the restrictive teachings of her church school and prudish parents.

He muttered curses to himself as he thought of what she'd been through then the reality of what was happening to her now hit him like a cold shower.

The thought of her in danger—physical or emotional danger—was like an arrow pricking at his heart, arousing the strong protective feelings he hadn't felt since Charlotte's birth.

He'd take her home, he'd keep her safe—

Imprison her? a snide voice in his head whispered.

No, that wasn't love.

Now, where the hell had love come into it?

Wasn't he the man who'd sworn off love?

He pulled into the co-op car park, pleased that thoughts of food could push the other confusing issues to the back of his head.

They ate on the deck, Buddy, who'd been imprisoned in his cage while they'd slept, taking great delight in hopping between them.

'Who knew you had a galah?'

Will's question brought Alex out of her pleasant daze and she frowned at him.

'Why?'

He answered her frown with a smile that made her nerves twitch—again!

'Because whoever left the bird outside knew,' he said, serious now, the words squelching twitching nerves very effectively.

She tried to think—think back.

'Friends from school?' Will prompted, but Alex shook her head.

'Some, maybe,' she said. 'Caitlin Kerr was my best friend, so I'd have told her when I got him, and if you think about it, she could have told anyone. So could Mum and Dad. But only Caitlin ever stayed over. Her family went to the same church as mine, so my parents liked her.'

Had her voice quavered that Will reached out and took her hand?

'I know you don't want it to be this Caitlin—that would be too much of a betrayal—but can you think of any reason why all that happened would have hurt her?'

'No, and no, and no! Caitlin was the only person from the school who ever got in touch with me. She was at the trial one day—not inside but waiting outside the court—and she pressed a letter into my hand then rushed away.

She said she believed me and how sorry she was, but she couldn't risk her parents' anger by seeing me again.'

'She believed you?'

Alex found a rueful smile, although memories of that time still caused deep pain.

'At least someone did—apart from Dave and Isobel, of course.'

'And me, I never doubted you,' Will assured her, before moving on.

'So Caitlin has to be a starting point. She believed you so if we find her, maybe she'd be willing to talk to us about what happened after you left town—or after the court case. She might even know who would have been most upset.'

'Mrs Spencer, I would say to that,' Alex offered, 'but I can't see her even thinking a swear word, let alone spray-painting it on someone's house. She was very godly and so shadowy she was barely there. And anyway, the Spencers left town.'

'How do you know that?'

Alex had to think, then it came back to her.

'Would you believe one of the nurses at the hospital? Apparently, there were more people than I realised who thought I'd told the truth, and her family was one of them.'

'So, we'll talk to her as well. Can you remember her name?'

Alex shook her head.

'I should be able to, but it's gone. Anyway, she's in the CCU so I'll be able to find her. Maybe Robyn.'

'Robyn Alcorn, she's a wonderful person—I'm sure she'd be happy to talk to us. What time is it?'

Alex glanced at her watch, surprised to find it was mid-afternoon.

'You're not going looking for her now, are you?' she asked.

'The sooner the better,' Will declared. 'Although I want you to pack up some clothes. You can stay with me—well, in Mum's flat—until it's sorted.'

Alex shook her head.

'I'm sorry, Will, but I won't do that. Everything is moving just too fast. I need some time to come to terms not just with the stalking but with...'

She balked, and Will squeezed her fingers and smiled the smile that made her heart ache.

'With you and me?'

'Especially with you and me, because it isn't just you and me, is it? It's you and Charlotte as well, and if I mess this up, and I could, then I wouldn't want her getting—I don't know, perhaps confused about the situation.'

The words hit Will like a slap across the head with a wet fish! What on earth was he thinking—where was his brain?—that he'd completely left Charlotte out of the equation when he'd suggested Alex move in with his mother?

Then there was the fact that maybe Alex didn't want a stepdaughter and her talk of messing things up was a way of telling him that...

She reached out and took his hand.

'It can't possibly be as bad as whatever you're thinking,' she said gently. 'All I'm saying is that this is very new and we don't want to rush things.'

He took a deep breath to allay the panic that had been fluttering in his head and in his heart—and obviously on his face!

'Okay,' he said. 'But as Mum and Charlotte are away until Tuesday, I'll stay tonight and first thing tomorrow we get a security firm here and have alarms installed—

alarms and sensor lights and whatever else the experts recommend.'

He stood up and pulled her to him, holding her loosely in the cradle of his arms.

'I can understand your need to be here—to let the house become your home again—but *I* need you to be safe.'

A different warmth flooded Alex now and she kissed this man who'd brought such unexpected pleasure into her life. Not that his next suggestion was all pleasure.

'We have to do it, Alex,' he said gently, when she protested about sitting down to write a list of all her parents' friends, her friends, and even neighbours they'd had in the past.

'It's been twenty years,' she reminded him.

'Which only makes it worse,' he said, with a gravity she'd not heard before. 'Someone who has nurtured such hatred for twenty years is not entirely sane.'

Alex shivered at the thought, but found a pad and pen and sat down, putting Caitlin at the top of the list.

'I'll get my tablet from the car,' Will suggested. 'We can check if any of the people you remember are still at their old addresses and get phone numbers.'

'Wouldn't a phone book be just as easy?' Alex smiled as she said it, and smiled even more widely when he admitted it probably would work well.

The Kerrs were listed at their old address, which immediately presented a new dilemma.

'Do I ring and ask for a number for Caitlin?' Alex said, dread at the thought gripping at her stomach.

'Better I do it. Let's think of a reasonable excuse.'

But in the end Will didn't have to use any excuse.

'We no longer speak her name in this house,' the man who answered the phone said, and hung up.

'Well, that went well!' Will said. 'Perhaps we stick to lists and then we track down Robyn and get her to tell us what she can about the people on it.'

Alex tried, but after jotting down some names of her parents' friends then girls she'd been close to at school, she pushed the pad away.

'You know,' she muttered, 'writing out a list of people who might hate you is not the most cheerful thing to be doing on a Sunday afternoon. Let's take the bird to the police station then you can show me where you live while you get a few things for the night.'

She must have sounded even more depressed than she felt for he agreed immediately, once again hauling her out of her chair and holding her in his arms.

Which, inevitably perhaps, led to other things, and it was much later that she locked a loudly protesting Buddy in his cage and they left the house.

First stop the hospital, to check on their joint patient, only semi-conscious as yet, but the monitors showed he was doing well.

'This wasn't where you used to live,' she said, when Will pulled up in front of a modern-looking house that was tucked against the cliff and looked out over the ocean.

'No, Mum moved after Elise and I were married,' he explained. 'That's what made this so convenient. I don't know if you remember the old house, but it would have been impossible to convert it to two flats. Whereas here we not only had the land, but the beach is right there for Charlotte.'

Charlotte!

Definitely the pivotal point in Will's life!

And suddenly something about entering his flat—seeing toys and other evidence of Charlotte—held Alex back.

Failure at relationships with men was one thing, but if she failed in a relationship with a child?

'No, I'll wait in the car. The view is lovely.'

Extremely weak, but he didn't argue so maybe he'd realised it was too early to get too involved.

'I'll just grab some clean clothes and a toothbrush,' he said, although he did kiss her swiftly on the cheek before he got out of the car.

She was asleep when Will returned, and he stood and looked at the miracle that had come into his life—the miracle that was Alex.

He didn't want to think too far into the future, something about this relationship was too fragile for that, but just seeing her there, relaxed in sleep, filled him with inexplicable joy.

Could they make this work?

Could *he* make it work?

He'd loved Elise deeply and completely, to the extent that her death had nearly destroyed him. It had been only the little scrap of humanity that was Charlotte that had kept him going—her and surfing, because out there on the ocean he could cry...

But what he felt for Alex was different—it had an element of physical passion he'd never known before.

Could such passion last?

And if it didn't, wasn't Alex right about not wanting Charlotte hurt in the fallout?

And what of hurting Alex?

If the relationship failed, she'd blame herself!

He looked through the window at the beautiful woman sleeping in his car, doubts and memories jumbling in his head.

The one thing he *did* know was that Alex had been hurt enough in the past and, whatever the future held, there was no way he could hurt her again.

Should he walk away now?

He shook his head as he went to get behind the wheel.

No way could he walk away now—not when she was still under threat.

Not when he loved her?

He frowned at the random question thrown up by his brain.

Love?

So quickly?

No way!

His love for Elise had grown like a seedling, spindly and unsure at first but strengthening over time as they'd grown to know each other.

This was different—so different…

Enough!

He stood by the car door to phone the hospital, hoping to track down Robyn Alcorn and enlist her help in finding out who might want to harm Alex.

Alex opened her eyes and gazed around her. She was in a car with the sea beyond the windows.

Outside Will's house.

She could hear his voice—muffled, outside the car—talking on the phone?

She sat up, suddenly very awake and smiling at her memories of the day.

'Robyn's on days off,' Will announced, opening the car door and slinging an overnight bag into the back seat.

'She'll be on duty on Wednesday, so we'll stick to making the list and have it ready when we talk to her then.'

Alex wanted to protest—that making the list was too hard, too hurtful—but she knew he was right.

'Are you always this masterful?' she asked, smiling at him as he reminded her to fasten her seat belt.

'Always,' he said firmly, leaning across to give her a kiss. 'Police station next, then home to your place. Do you need to do any shopping on the way?'

Not only masterful but domesticated.

Domesticated by his mother or Elise?

The reality of his first wife struck her suddenly, and she wondered how much of a factor a dead wife could be in a relationship. She'd been too caught up in thinking about the effect of the relationship on a child—

If there *was* a relationship!

Maybe it was all too complicated, right from the beginning, and now was the time to back away.

The thoughts were only tiny darts pricking at her senses, but they were still there.

Except when she looked at Will, saw the little smile hovering on his lips, the gleam in his eyes when he glanced towards her...

No, she had to find out what lay ahead—be it good or bad.

She had to give her all to this relationship, if only to prove that she *could* make one work!

She reached out and rested her hand on Will's thigh, and smiled back when he turned to smile at her.

CHAPTER NINE

WAKING IN THE morning with a man in her bed felt strange to Alex, strange but wonderful. But Will was obviously a morning person—no doubt because of Charlotte—soon up and about, making cups of tea, bringing them, with the phone, back to bed with him.

A little lost in the newness of it all—the unfamiliarity—Alex looked out at the river, sipping her tea, doubts about the rightness of the situation still niggling at her. The sex was new and wonderful, but was that casting a rosy glow over everything else?

Making her think love?

Making her think it could make a difference in a relationship—maybe make it work?

'Ha, just what we want—a twenty-four seven security service. I'll phone them now.'

Will's small cry of triumph made her forget her doubts and concentrate on the present.

His phone was by his wallet—the wallet from which he'd extracted a couple of condoms—and within seconds he was arranging for someone to be at the house as soon as possible.

'So, you'll have to get up and put some clothes on,' he told Alex, smiling down at her. 'Not that I don't like you exactly the way you are.'

The smile, his cheeriness should have reassured her, but a feeling that things had moved too fast still clung to the edges of her mind. He was out of the room before she could put it into words—although she probably couldn't anyway. It was nothing more than a slight uneasiness…

Thoroughly pleased with his efforts so far this morning, Will explored the refrigerator.

'How about an omelette?' he called up to Alex, needing to keep busy because he was still uneasy about the situation. Nothing he could put his finger on—Alex was wonderful, beautiful and sexy and great company, and he suspected he was already in love with her.

He who hadn't wanted love…

But the suddenness, and Charlotte, and losing Elise the way he had, threw shadows on his happiness.

'So keep busy,' he told himself, shooing Buddy away from the eggs he was beating. 'We'll have breakfast then do the list, whether Alex wants to or not, and later maybe go out on the river again—go further up, explore…'

Alex—even thinking her name brought a surge of desire.

Maybe they wouldn't go up the river later…

She wandered into the kitchen, wrapped in a purple kimono, hair tousled and face slightly flushed.

'Are you really this domesticated?' she asked, as he grated cheese then chopped some tomatoes.

'Well trained,' he said. 'Four years of bachelorhood, remember, and a child to feed. I had to learn to feed the pair of us, although I've always cooked. Elise would have fed us on lamb chops, mashed potato and peas every night of the week—cooking was never her thing.'

His gut clenched as soon as the words were out. Was mentioning Elise a good or bad thing?

But she'd existed—she was Charlotte's birth mother—

so surely if she came into the conversation naturally, some of the awkwardness he guessed Alex was feeling might dissipate.

'Well, I'm glad you cook, for whatever reason,' Alex told him, coming closer to kiss his cheek. 'Because most Sunday mornings I just laze around and probably don't eat at all until lunchtime. You'd have been starving by then.'

She started the coffee-machine while he cooked the omelette, dividing it onto two plates, adding a little of the chilli sauce he'd found in the pantry.

They ate on the deck, and the strain he'd felt earlier seemed to drift off in the soft spring air, Alex smiling as he fed Buddy a very small piece of his breakfast.

'He'll drive you mad now, begging at every meal,' Alex teased, and a certainty that this was right for him—for both of them—banished the rest of his doubts.

He took Alex's hand in his.

'I hope there will be many meals for him to drive me mad at,' he said quietly, and knew she understood when colour rose in her cheeks and she squeezed his fingers in hers.

'I hope so too,' she whispered. 'I really do!'

And she was pretty sure she meant it.

Loud knocking at the door finished the conversation.

'Security man!' Will said.

Alex leapt to her feet, gathering up their plates and mugs.

'I'll have to put some clothes on. I didn't think he'd be this quick!'

She took the dirty dishes to the kitchen and dashed upstairs, leaving Will to open the door.

Security, she discovered, wasn't a simple matter of putting in an alarm. Once told of the problems she'd been having, the specialist insisted on CCTV cameras outside the house, one covering both street approaches and one at the side of the house where the power box was.

'We can take that one away later,' he said, 'after the perpetrator has been caught. But it will be handy to have it there for now because most people believe if you turn off the power then the alarms won't work so we would get a close-up of whoever it is who is pestering you. We'll conceal them as best we can and do as much as we can today when a stalker is less likely to be around.'

Bemused by all the technological marvels he was suggesting and his obvious knowledge of problem situations, Alex just nodded, going along with what he was suggesting because not taking notice of an expert would be stupid.

'It'll be costly,' the man said, and she shook her head.

'Doesn't matter,' she told him at the same time as Will offered to pay. 'Nonsense, it's my house and my security, and as I'll have to have a base in town for nights when I'm working late, it will be good to have the place secure.'

With a promise that work would begin within an hour, and a substantial deposit, the man departed.

'Back to the list,' Will said, and something in his voice told her he meant it.

But the list was impossible! The three couples she'd considered closest to her parents no longer had addresses in the phone book, neither could they be found on Will's tablet—well, not with any certainty.

'They all had children so I suppose if the children moved away the parents might have followed once grandchildren came along.'

'We'll put them on the list anyway,' Will insisted. 'Robyn might know something about them.'

So Alex obediently wrote them down.

'Now, schoolfriends other than Caitlin,' he said, and Alex listed the names of classmates with whom she'd been close—and others she only vaguely remembered.

'Other people at the church—the hierarchy who stood by Spencer at the time?' Will persisted.

Alex shook her head.

'It's all a blur, that time, Will. I don't know if I've deliberately deleted it all from my memory or if I was just so stressed back then that nothing stuck.'

'That's okay. I'm sure the police can search out the files and see if there was anyone who stood out as particularly hurt by the business.'

'Apart from poor Mrs Spencer,' Alex muttered.

Will pushed the list away, took her hand, and said, 'How about that boat ride?'

As Alex opened the door to the boatshed beneath the house she saw the kayak.

'Better still, let's try the kayak. Can you paddle one?'

Kayak!

Tony Mitchell!

Will felt a faint uneasiness in his stomach that he was pretty sure wasn't the omelette.

'I've been in one,' he said carefully, hoping his uneasiness wasn't jealousy.

'Then show me how,' Alex demanded, and although he'd have liked to say that surely she wouldn't still be joining the kayak club, he knew that was nothing more than selfishness. Alex needed to build a life back in her home town—a life for herself, not just a life with him, and that was if the 'life with him' thing worked out.

But he still felt majorly grouchy as he carried the kayak down to the water, holding it carefully while he stepped precariously into it.

'Shouldn't you have a life-jacket on?' Alex asked.

'Of course I should, but all I'm doing is a little "here's how to do it" paddle right in close to the shore. I can stand up in the water here.'

Why was she doing this? Alex wondered, as she watched Will settle into a rhythm with the single oar, digging it in one side then the other.

Because you need a life apart from Will, the sensible part of her brain reminded her.

However you might feel about him, there's still a lot of uncertainty there, and, given your propensity to muck up relationships, you have to make friends to fall back on.

She knew the sensible voice in her head was spot on, but seeing Will smiling as the art of kayaking came back to him she knew that this time she would do her darnedest to make the relationship work!

'We can both join the kayak club,' she told him, as he held the little craft steady for her to climb in.

'We'll see,' was all he replied, and although she'd have liked to analyse the tone of the words, she was too busy trying to stay out of the river, the kayak seeming to tip dangerously every time she moved.

'It won't tip,' Will assured her. 'Just get comfortable and then try the paddle.'

'Get comfortable when it's going to buck me into the water any minute?' Alex shrieked.

'It won't, I'm still holding it.'

She glanced around and Will was still there, waist deep in water now but still holding the flimsy craft as steady as he could.

'You really didn't have to get wet,' she protested, and he smiled and what she could only assume was love surged through her.

'I wanted to be sure you were safe,' he said simply, then the smile slid away and he added, 'Always.'

Her heart stopped beating—only for a moment—but something about that simple declaration had touched her as nothing else ever had.

It *had* to be love!

But how to handle it, how to nurture it and help it grow...

She lifted the paddle and imitated Will's movements earlier.

'Let go,' she said. 'I have to do this on my own!'

A bit like love, the doing-it-on-your-own thing.

Sure, you could share it with the loved one and that shared love needed care and attention too—but the love in your heart?

How did you protect that?

And if you couldn't, just how badly would it hurt?

But somehow she was paddling, still in the shallows at the river edge. The thoughts of love racing through her head must have helped the rhythm, and the feeling was great.

Until she tried to turn to go back to where Will waited. The disaster she was coming to expect from all her personal endeavours came as the kayak tipped her unceremoniously into the river and she emerged, dripping, the paddle clutched in one hand, the kayak in the other.

'You did well to grab them both. Most first-timers lose one or the other,' Will said, mostly, Alex suspected, to cover the fact that he was laughing at her.

Or with her?

Because now she was laughing too, both of them saturated, Will towing the kayak back to her beach while she slogged through the water in her sodden clothes.

'Now we'll *have* to shower together,' Will told her, as

seeing her body through the wet material sent a surge of desire through his.

'I guess so,' Alex replied, and together they returned the kayak and its paddle to the shed, but when they entered the house, intending to strip off their wet clothing before going further, they realised three men from the security firm were there, and even if they showered together, they could hardly make love while the men were prowling around.

'Another time,' Will whispered in her ear, and they squelched upstairs, Alex directing Will to the main bathroom while she sought refuge in her new en suite.

The phone was ringing as she came out—the hospital, to say Adam Hawkins had been admitted.

Not wanting to leave before speaking to Will, she waited until he returned from his shower.

'Adam Hawkins,' she said. 'He's been admitted to hospital.'

'He's the lad I was telling you about earlier—the one waiting for a new heart. You've met him?'

'Thursday. I'd been reading his file and wanted to see how he was doing on the portable IV infusions, and check he was getting enough support from the community nurses. I know his GP monitors him, but, well, I suppose I wanted to meet him.'

Will checked his pager.

'He'll have been admitted to the ICU but no one's paged me so I assume Josh Turner's coping with the situation.'

'He's not in the ICU, he's in Theatre—they've found a heart and it's being flown in as we speak.'

Alex's own heart was racing. She'd stood in as an extra surgeon once in Glasgow but somehow here, with Adam her patient, it was different.

'I've got to go,' she told Will, aware there'd be a full anaesthetic team in Theatre and Will wouldn't be needed until after the op.

'I know,' he said, and he took her face in her hands. 'You'll do brilliantly, the lot of you, and know I'll be thinking of you all the time.'

He dropped a kiss on her lips, a kiss of such sweetness her mind, as she drove, kept drifting back to it when she should have been concentrating on what lay ahead for Adam and how much the cardiovascular surgeons would call on her to help.

Making her way swiftly to the ICU when she arrived at the hospital, Alex realised just how quickly she'd settled in, and how easily she'd been accepted by the staff.

She headed straight for the main theatre, to find Adam already on the table. Well, she assumed it was Adam as he was totally covered except for his bony chest, which had already been cut open, and held agape by clamps. The diseased heart flopped about in his chest like a deflated balloon, moving a little as it tried to keep working.

She watched as Norm Wright, who apparently had the lead role in the procedure, attached a cannula to the vena cava, slid a tube into place in the cannula, turned on a switch on the bypass machine and watched as Adam's blood drained into it. The return cannula had already been inserted into the patient's aorta so blood was now flowing through Adam's body but completely bypassing his heart.

The donor heart had been removed from its cooler bag and the vessels to be attached to Adam's vessels neatly trimmed. The surgeons swiftly severed Adam's heart and carefully, with minute stitches, attached Adam's veins and arteries to the new ones.

Finally, the job was done and the moment of truth had

arrived. Norm detached the tube from the cannula and unclamped the aorta. Now warm blood from the heart-lung machine began to flow into the new heart—the icy-cold organ not long emerged from the cooler.

The strain in the room was palpable, Alex as stiff and silent as the rest. Norm's assistant reached into Adam's chest and gave the new heart a couple of gentle squeezes.

Nothing.

He repeated the procedure and this time it worked. The shiny new undamaged heart remembered its job and began to beat. Relief flowed through the team but the job wasn't done. Now Norm inserted a tiny electrode that would keep the new heart beating at ninety-nine beats a minute for a few days until it picked up the rhythm on its own.

Norm and his assistant stepped back.

'Dr Hudson, would you like to close?'

Pleased to be part of something so wonderful—apart from passing a clamp or two—Alex moved forward eagerly. Drawing the sides of the sternum back together, she fixed them with wire, then began the tedious stitching up of the skin, layer by layer, until Adam's chest looked as if it had been zipped back together.

Having been part of the final surgery, she accompanied her patient back to the recovery room, although he was now in the care of the anaesthetists until he regained consciousness.

The anaesthetists and Will, who was waiting in Recovery, anxious to know how the operation had gone and to check Adam's status, for he'd be Will's patient in Intensive Care for the next little while.

Alex's heart warmed at the sight of him, and she answered his raised eyebrows with a broad smile and a thumbs-up.

But exhaustion was creeping in and as Will spoke to the anaesthetists she slipped away, past Norm Wright, who was talking to Adam's anxious but cautiously optimistic parents, and into the locker room to shower and change.

Change!

Taking it literally, she couldn't but think how much change there'd been in her life in the last few weeks.

Coming home, her father's death—and Will!

Standing under the shower, she tried to sort through her thoughts. Coming home had been the right thing to do—she knew that now and not only because of Will. Her father's death—that was strange. She felt she should be grieving more for the man who'd done so much to make up for the past, but as she pondered her reactions she realised the tears she'd shed had been over little things—kindnesses she hadn't hoped for.

And, gradually, she realised that she'd grieved for her lost parents a long time ago—and probably for too long—although time was really the only healer for grief.

Her father's gifts—especially the Anzac biscuits—made her feel he was still around, the kindly man she'd known as a child, and somehow she knew that now he'd always be with her...

She went into the small office beside the theatres and wrote up her notes of the operation. The surgeons' notes would be more comprehensive, but Adam was Brian's patient—her patient now—and needed the record.

Will appeared when she was closing down the computer.

'I need to get out of here for a while,' she said to him. 'The ferry starts at dawn so I'll go home, check on Buddy then come back to check on Adam before I go to the rooms.'

'Good idea, but you'll need to take these.'

Will handed her a couple of keys and a card with numbers written on it.

'These are the keys for the new deadbolt the security people put on the front door and the card has the numbers for the security system. The keypad for it is in the hall, and you just key in the numbers to deactivate the alarm.'

'Oh, great!' Alex muttered. 'I put in the wrong numbers and wake the entire neighbourhood at five in the morning.'

Will closed her fingers around the keys and squeezed her hand.

'You won't key in the wrong numbers,' he told her, his dark eyes serious for once. 'Just drive carefully. I mean it, Alex, because I'd hate anything to happen to you.'

It wasn't exactly a declaration of love but, standing at the desk in the ICU when a young patient had been given a new chance at life, it sounded like one, and it was only with the greatest difficulty that Alex refrained from kissing him there and then.

She made do with a husky, 'I'll be fine. I'll come back here—see you—before I go to work, okay?'

He nodded and gave her fingers a final squeeze. She was walking away when he called quietly, 'Go out the main entrance not the one near the car park.'

She turned back, aware that she was frowning at the suggestion.

'Why?'

'Media! They hear stuff by osmosis and Adam's fight and his wait on the list for a new heart has been widely publicised. They'll be looking for someone to comment at the staff entrance.'

Now he smiled at her as he added, 'Port is still a small town at heart.'

The smile filled her with warmth and she walked away with a lighter step.

Will watched her disappear from the unit and shook his head at the speed with which his life had turned around. For all his doubts about allowing any woman, let alone Alex, into his life, somehow it had happened.

Yes, it had been sudden, and the suddenness had made him wary at first, worried that it might be nothing more than a physical attraction. But the more time he'd spent with her the more certain he'd become that he wanted her in his life for ever.

But his life included Charlotte's life.

Was Alex ready to meet her?

Was *he* ready to introduce her to Charlotte?

He saw Adam Hawkins's parents perched outside the ICU.

'You know when he gets in there, it's only one at a time, and then only for a few minutes. The operation was a major stress on his body and he needs to recover from it.'

They nodded, understanding, but needing to be near, even if it was only outside in the corridor.

'You know Adam's courage and his personality while he waited for a heart has made him a local hero, which means the press will be after you for stories.'

'Of course they will,' Mrs Hawkins answered for Will. 'After all, it was the press and their stories that helped raise the money we've needed for him over the years, and made people aware of the importance of organ donation. But…'

She looked beseechingly at Will.

'Could the hospital do it for us? Have a press conference? Just tell them Adam's got his new heart and now
we can only wait and see.'

She paused, then added, 'We'll be able to talk about
it in a little while, but just now...'

She broke off with a tremulous smile and Will understood that she didn't want to hope too much—didn't want
to believe in a miracle until she saw her son's recovery
with her own eyes.

'But we really don't want to talk to anyone right now,'
Mr Hawkins added, his voice breaking with loss and
strain.

'I'll sort it all out,' Will promised, although he did
wish Brian Lane could be here to take the conference
with the hospital media boss and Norm Wright, the cardiovascular surgeon. In Brian's absence, Alex would have
to do it. It wasn't that he doubted she'd manage—she'd
probably done dozens of similar conferences in the past.

But back in the town where the media had crucified
her?

Although that was so long ago, did it matter?

He assured himself it didn't but the assurance failed
to settle a knot of tension in his gut.

She'll be fine, he assured himself, and, later on, as
he stood at the back of the room and watched, he found
she was, answering the questions put to her with a poise
and confidence that replaced the tension he'd been feeling with enormous pride.

One more night together then, Will had decided,
he'd spend his spare time for the rest of the week with
Charlotte, making up for time they'd missed.

But also mentioning Alex?

He wasn't sure.

He'd talk to his mother.

Talk to Alex first to be certain she'd agree to meet his daughter the following weekend.

CHAPTER TEN

OFFICIALLY ON A day off after a week on call, Will finished early and went home to have a sleep. Guilt that he was sleeping while Alex worked didn't last long and he woke refreshed and full of plans.

He'd collect her from her work and drive her home, organise a meal delivery so they could eat and go to bed early.

His body stirred at the 'go to bed early' idea but he dismissed it. They needed to talk, if only while they ate their dinner, and Alex would be tired.

He phoned her rooms to ask Marilyn to pass on this plan, no longer caring who knew about him and Alex. Not that Marilyn seemed at all surprised.

Hospitals! Word spread like wildfire through them.

Alex smiled as she looked at the message slip Marilyn had passed her.

'Lover-boy will collect you after work, and organise dinner,' it read, and she knew the cheeky note showed that the office manager had accepted her.

And Will!

As a couple?

Wasn't it too soon?

'Just go with the flow,' she said to herself, speaking out loud to give the words emphasis.

'What flow?' the patient who'd followed her into the room asked, and Alex smiled.

'Any old flow, I suppose,' she said, smiling at the man who'd already taken a seat.

'The nurse checked my heart—does she send the printout from the machine to you on your computer?' he asked.

'She does indeed,' Alex told him, bringing up his file. 'And your heart is looking very healthy. The stents Dr Lane arranged to have put in are working well, and, from your blood-test results, your blood pressure and this ECG, I would say you're fine.'

She'd stood up and approached her patient as she was speaking, wanting to listen to his chest. He knew the routine well enough to pull up his shirt, and when she was done he thanked her, pulled down his shirt, then said, 'You don't remember me, do you?'

Alex shook her head. Wainwright, the patient's name was Wainwright.

'I remember you as a little kid, always out in that tinnie you had,' he said. 'I had a trawler down at the co-op docks and you once asked me if I'd pay you for yabbies.'

Alex smiled, although his earlier mention of the past had sent an icy shiver down her spine.

Now the smile was genuine as she remembered happy times.

'You told me you used nets and didn't need bait,' she said, and Mr Wainwright laughed.

'You must have been all of seven and you told me you were saving up for a car—a red car. Did you ever get it?'

'I did eventually,' Alex told him, the smile slipping off her face as she thought of how she'd come by her red car.

'Well, it's good to see you,' Mr Wainwright said, pushing himself to his feet. 'Do I still have to come back for a check-up in three months?'

'I think for a fellow fisherman I could make it six, unless your GP decides to send you back to me.'

They shook hands and Alex walked out with her patient, and was surprised to see the waiting room empty.

'What's happened?' she asked the receptionist at the desk. 'Did you spray some kind of patient repellent around?'

The young woman laughed. 'No, but Dr Kent told Marilyn how you'd been up all night with Adam, so she contacted your last two patients and also let Dr Kent know you'd be finishing early.'

So now everyone knows about us, Alex thought, seeing the knowing smile on the receptionist's face.

As Will had said, Port still had the heart of a small town.

Will!

They talked very little on the drive home, Alex content just to be near him. But once on the ferry she turned to him and smiled.

'Thank you for doing this—I *was* too tired to drive, and probably too tired to get the numbers right on my new security system.'

'Worry not, for Superman is here,' he said, leaning across to kiss her cheek before putting the vehicle into gear to drive off.

It made her laugh but as he drove the short distance to her home she studied the man who'd not only brought laughter into her life but had also taught her how to love.

Because it had to be love, the warmth inside her, the slightly dizzy way she felt when she was with him, and the way her nerves tightened and her toes curled when he smiled at her...

So she stood close to him as he disarmed the alarm and sat close to him on the deck as they had a drink and ate the dinner he'd ordered.

They talked about her day, about Adam and his parents, about everything and nothing, although Alex knew it was chat.

'So, what is it you want to say?' she finally asked, and her heart squeezed tight when Will hesitated.

'It's about Charlotte,' he admitted. 'I need to spend any spare time I have with her this week, but I'm off duty next weekend and I wondered...'

He stared out across the river at the lights of the houses opposite then looked towards the centre of the town—towards his house and his family.

'Wondered?' Alex prompted, although she was sure she knew what was coming.

'Wondered if you'd like to do something with us. Go to the beach or the park or just have breakfast at the surf club, or maybe I could make dinner at my place, or—'

Alex pressed her fingers to his lips.

'I do get it,' she told him. 'You want me to meet Charlotte and, more importantly, her to meet me.'

She hoped she sounded more composed than she felt, because this was it, the test.

It wouldn't be about Charlotte liking her—that wouldn't happen until they knew each other better and Charlotte was assured Alex wouldn't steal her father.

No, it was about commitment, and whether the feelings she had for Will were real enough to be a strong foundation for a family—Will, Charlotte and herself.

And later...

The thought of having Will's baby spread sheer happiness through her body, but she'd leapt too far ahead.

And Will was talking again, his nerves obvious as he

practically babbled about it being up to her, and how he didn't want to foist Charlotte on her, and—

This time she stopped him with a kiss.

'It's okay,' she said, when they broke apart. 'You decide how best you want to do it and I'll fit in. Perhaps you'd like to bring her here, we could go out in the tinnie. Dad always kept a couple of little life-jackets for the neighbours' kids or grandkids, and Buddy's good with kids—he seems to like them, lets them pat him and sits on their shoulders.'

'Oh, Alex,' he said, and he put his arms around her, hauling her to her feet so he could kiss her properly. 'That would be wonderful!'

The kiss deepened, which led to moving like some clumsy four-legged animal up the stairs and into the room by the river.

Alex pushed herself away, excitement overcoming her tiredness.

'I need to shower,' she said. 'I won't be long.'

She saw Will's face and saw some of the uncertainty that had been in his words earlier.

Very carefully, she took his hand and led him into the bathroom, slowly stripping off his clothes, letting him remove hers, hoping he'd understand this act of showering together was her commitment to him.

Understand that she loved him!

There, it was out, no more dithering. What she felt for Will couldn't be anything but love, although in a shower with him, spreading soap across his body, enjoying the sensations when he returned the favour—well, some of that was lust...

To Will, her unspoken invitation to join him in the shower was a gift—the gift of trust, something he was certain Alex had never been able to give another man.

Will touched her gently, reverently, and when they made love beneath the water, he was speechless with an emotion he'd never felt before, yet wary that such happiness had come his way, aware how quickly happiness could be stripped away...

She fell asleep before him, curled into his body, and although he knew it would take time for Alex and Charlotte to get to know each other, he let himself dare to dream about the future—about family...

Alex woke, kissed the cheek of her still-sleeping lover, pulled on a robe and went downstairs to get the paper that her father must have organised to have delivered every day. Although at first she'd thought she'd cancel it, this morning she was glad she hadn't because today it would hold the end of Adam's story.

Disarming the alarm before she opened the door, pleased with herself for remembering the numbers, she slipped out, picked it up, then unfolded it as she walked back inside, wanting to see what was said.

'Oh!'

'What is it? What's wrong?'

Will was coming down the stairs and must have heard her involuntary exclamation.

'Nothing, it's just... I didn't think...'

Her voice trailed off when she couldn't find the words she needed, so she handed the paper to Will, pointing at the picture that topped the lead story—a picture of her, Norm and the hospital's media expert.

'It should have been a picture of Adam, not us,' she finally managed, disturbed by the exposure, though unable to explain why.

'You can never tell what the press will do,' Will said. 'And, anyway, it's a great picture of you. Norm, they've made to look like a mad scientist—they took it when he put on his glasses to read the official statement.'

Alex had another look and had to smile—Norm did look like a mad scientist—but her uneasiness remained, staying with her all day, while patients praised the picture or talked about Adam, intensifying as she drove home.

She sat in her car on the ferry, wanting to phone Will but not wanting to break into his time with Charlotte.

She could text him—just say Miss U. That wouldn't interrupt too much—

Her phone buzzed—a text, the message she'd been sending in her head there on her phone.

She stared at it, then, with total inanity, kissed the plastic screen, although she didn't tell him that when he phoned later, after Charlotte was in bed, to tell her the same thing but in a lot more words.

For some reason she slept late. Dressing quickly, she skipped breakfast—one of the nurses would get her a coffee and muffin from the shop downstairs. She set the security alarm then raced out the door, grabbing the paper from her front lawn on her way to her car. She'd have a quick look at it on the ferry.

But Will phoned while she sat in the queue of vehicles, waiting to board, and the paper was forgotten.

Until he said, 'Have you seen the paper?'

'No, I'm going to read it on the ferry. Hang on a sec while I get the car on board.'

She negotiated her vehicle into the tight spot the ferry lad was showing her, morning traffic making the trip more difficult, then got back to the phone.

'Don't open the paper,' Will said. 'I'll meet you at your rooms. Come straight here, you can do a ward round later.'

'Don't open the paper?'

'Please, Alex, I'm asking this of you—just do it for me, okay?'

Totally bemused, she agreed, but as she drove off the ferry she glanced at the paper lying next to her handbag on the seat beside her and wondered what it could possibly contain that had Will so excited.

Or upset?

Yes, he'd sounded more upset than excited.

The drive to work was agonising, and several times she reached out to just sneak a look, but she'd promised— or kind of promised.

Missing her ward round meant she was now early to work, but Marilyn was already there, her face set in an expression Alex couldn't read, so when the efficient, unflappable woman burst into tears, Alex was at a total loss.

She stepped swiftly towards her and put her arms around Marilyn's shoulders.

'Whatever it is, it can't be *that* bad,' she said, but shook her head.

'It is, it is, and Will's told me all about it and it's so unfair but it will hurt the practice, I know it will.'

Someone's died and the relatives are blaming Brian or Mal, Alex guessed, so she gave Marilyn's shoulders an extra squeeze then said, 'You look like you could do with a decent coffee and I missed breakfast. Let's pop down to the canteen together for a muffin and a coffee. Do you want to freshen up first?'

Marilyn straightened up, sniffed back her tears and trotted off to the washroom to obliterate any sign of them, calling over her shoulder, 'Will's in your office.'

Great!

Now perhaps she'd learn what on earth was going on.

She headed down the passage that led to her office, surprised to hear Will's voice. He must have been speaking very loudly—yelling?—because the rooms, with thick walls and heavy doors, were fairly soundproof.

He stopped his conversation as Alex walked in so the last words she heard were, 'My lawyer will be in touch with you.'

His face was pale but bright spots of anger burned on his cheeks.

'What's wrong? Is it Charlotte? What's happened?' Alex asked, coming towards him, her arms out to hold him.

He stood up from her chair and pulled her close.

She could feel his chest rising and falling as if he was taking deep breaths to steady himself.

'Not Charlotte, but you, my darling,' he said, his lips in her hair, his hands pressing her to him. 'Obviously thwarted by the security measures at your house, your stalker has taken to the media.'

Alex pushed away from him.

'What on earth do you mean?'

As Will seemed to be unable to say whatever words were needed, Alex snatched the paper from the bag she'd dropped on a visitor's chair and opened it.

There, across the top of two columns on the front page, was the picture that had appeared the day before, with Will and the media rep blotted out, only her face remaining.

And under it the headline: *'Woman who ruined the life of a good man returns to Port.'*

The story recounted the tale of the trial and Mr Spencer's acquittal—the headlines from the following day—the huge *'ACQUITTED!'* headline that had haunted Alex for years inserted into the text. It told of her family's shame, hinted that her mother had died of humiliation and a broken heart, and went on to insinuate that she'd only returned to get what she could after her father's death.

Somehow, as she'd read, Alex had sunk down into her chair, and now, hands trembling, she put the paper on her desk and looked up at Will.

'Poor Brian,' she whispered. 'He'll have to come back and start his search for a replacement all over again.'

'Don't be ridiculous,' Will growled. 'We'll fight this, it's slander, or libel, whatever they call the one that's printed. And we'll find out now who did it, because there couldn't be two people in town who hate you this much. We have to fight, you can't just run away.'

Alex reached out and touched his arm.

'Will,' she said, her voice catching on the simple syllable, 'if it was only me I'd do as you say, get myself a lawyer and fight to the death, but it isn't only me. It's the practice and don't say it won't suffer because people tend to believe just about everything they read. And a fair number of the practice's patients are older people who will remember the fuss at the time. Once that man was acquitted, I was branded a liar as well as a slut. I'll contact Brian, get him to find a locum, and get out as quickly as I can.'

'And me?' Will said, and Alex dredged up a smile from the black, anguished turmoil inside her.

'Do you really think I could taint Charlotte and your mother with this nonsense? It doesn't matter what we do, how we fight—and, yes, I'll get around to fighting—mud sticks, Will, you know that. And I can't have it sticking to an innocent little girl—have parents of the other kids pointing at her at kindy next year, people avoiding your mother. I won't do it but this is home for you and your family. You'll stay here, find a mother for Charlotte, and live happily ever after.'

So far, she told herself, she'd managed okay, but when she added, 'I told you my relationships didn't last,' the enormity of the loss she was facing—the loss of love—hit her like a fist slamming into her stomach, and she doubled over, resting her head on the desk, glad she hadn't eaten breakfast as bile rose in her throat.

A soft tap at the door and Marilyn entered, bearing coffee and a muffin.

'I know how busy you are, so I popped down on my own. It might be a bit cold now,' she said, speaking as if she hadn't been in floods of tears a little earlier, 'because Robyn Alcorn—the nurse from the cardiac unit—phoned to tell me it was all lies in the paper. She's said she's already rung the paper and wants someone to interview her for the other side of the story.'

That tiny scrap of unexpected kindness was the last straw.

As Alex lifted her head to thank Marilyn, the tears she'd been holding back overflowed.

Grabbing for a tissue from the box on her desk, she wiped them away.

'See, one kind word and I burst into tears,' she said. 'Of course I can't keep working here.'

'But we need you,' Marilyn said. 'With Brian and Mal away, and, what's more, all the patients you've already seen are singing your praises, talking about how they looked you up online and saw the work you'd done in Glasgow and they all think they're lucky to have you here in Port.'

'But will they think that now?' Alex asked, pushing the coffee and muffin to the side of her desk as the smell of the offering was making her feel ill.

Or more ill!

Will had been standing by the desk, statue still since Alex had pointed out the repercussions for their relationship.

His body screamed denial even as a small, still-functioning part of his brain suggested she might be right— at least about the slur on Charlotte.

But he looked at the woman at the desk and knew he couldn't let her out of his life. They could move away— all of them—he thought with a burst of optimism, but immediately discounted the solution. Alex would always be aware of the dark shadow hovering over her.

It would taint their life—their happiness.

No, there was only one way to do this and that was to fight.

'I'll see you later,' he said, and walked away, wondering what they'd done with the list, pathetic though it was.

They'd left it on the bench in the kitchen, he realised, feeling in his pocket where the key Alex had insisted he take hadn't yet been slipped onto his keyring.

He'd done a ward round and Josh was on duty so he phoned the ward and told them he'd be away from the hospital for an hour and to page him if he was needed.

Once on the ferry he phoned Robyn Alcorn's mobile number, which Marilyn had given him. She agreed only too happily to meet him at the hospital.

'I mightn't be able to help much,' she said, 'but I'll do whatever I can. It's cruel and scandalous what they've done to that woman, and she's a really good doctor too— the town needs people like her. People with roots here so they won't always be wanting to move somewhere else.'

Satisfied he'd done what he could for the moment, Will concentrated on getting safely to Alex's house, battling the hot anger churning through his body.

* * *

'Can you get Brian on the phone for me?' Alex asked Marilyn when Will had left the room. 'I need to find out what he'd want me to do.'

'He'll want you to stay,' Marilyn said stoutly, although Alex suspected there was a shade of uncertainty in her voice.

And that uncertainty raised another question.

'Have any patients cancelled?'

Marilyn looked embarrassed. She shrugged her shoulders, but as Alex held her eyes she finally admitted, 'A couple said they'd rather see Brian or Mal and made new appointments in a couple of weeks. No one knew Brian might not have been back, you see.'

Alex sighed.

'So, do I have any patients? Perhaps not everyone gets the paper.'

'Of course you've got patients,' Marilyn said. 'Don't worry, we'll keep you busy, and being busy you won't have time to think about all this rubbish.'

Although 'this rubbish' is what I'll have to think about, Alex thought, but there was no point in saying it out loud.

She made it through the day, most of her patients not mentioning the newspaper article, and the ones who did were angry about newspapers dredging up old scandals.

'As if it matters what happened twenty years ago,' one elderly woman said, 'and from what I heard, acquitted or not, that man was no good!'

Brian, when contacted, had said he'd return within a few days, but for support, nothing else—he wanted her to stay.

By the end of the day she was so physically and emotionally wrung out that even the ferry crossing failed to soothe her.

Arriving home, she looked in surprise at the huge bunch of bright flowers on her kitchen bench, and the note, a simple 'I love you', sitting beside it.

So Will had been here...

Just to leave flowers?

Alex looked around and realised the list was missing.

She had to smile—Superman springing into action on her behalf?—but she knew it was all too late. Whatever happened, some mud would stick and he and his daughter deserved better than that.

She opened the refrigerator and looked at the contents, Buddy perched on her shoulder, expecting a treat. It had been more than a week since she'd shopped and most things in there were looking a little tired and definitely uninspiring.

The freezer offered some ready-made meals that only needed a quick zap in the microwave but none of them appealed.

The phone rang as she was still peering into the freezer, hoping for inspiration.

A reporter, asking if she'd like to comment on the article.

'Wouldn't my comment have been more appropriate before you printed it rather than after?' she snapped, and slammed the phone back down.

At least in a town this size, with only one newspaper and no local television, she wouldn't be hounded by the press.

Deciding she wasn't hungry, she sank down onto one of the kitchen stools, rested her chin on her hand and gazed at her flowers, uncertain whether to smile or weep.

CHAPTER ELEVEN

Noises outside—a car pulling up.

Deciding there wasn't anyone in the world she wanted to see—well, apart from Will but it wouldn't be him—she had every intention of ignoring the expected ring on the doorbell.

But there was no ring, just the sound of a key in the lock, and although she knew, really, really knew she shouldn't get excited about Will being here, her heart leapt in her chest then hammered like a wild thing.

'Anyone home?' he called. 'You on the deck, Alex? You've got visitors.'

Visitors?

Plural?

She turned to see Will striding into the kitchen, a curly-headed moppet perched on one arm, and what looked like half a dozen shopping bags dangling from his other hand.

'I'd told Charlotte all about Buddy and she wanted to meet him,' he said brightly. 'And I've brought takeaway.'

Again! Alex thought, but that was only because she didn't want to think about the ramifications of this visit.

Buddy, meanwhile, was showing obvious delight to have a small person visiting him, bouncing up and down on the bench and going through his entire vocabulary, starting with the inevitable question about Bruce, telling Charlotte what a pretty girl she was, and finally finishing with such a wuss.

Charlotte was clearly delighted, looking at Alex with her father's sparkling brown eyes.

'Daddy said he could talk,' she said, kicking herself free of her father's arms and standing next to the bench, holding out a tentative hand towards the still-talking bird.

'Sometimes he talks too much,' Alex responded, her heart aching as she saw just what she'd be losing—this beautiful, trusting child, as well as Will.

'Look, Daddy, he's hopping up my arm.'

Her delight was so obvious Alex had to smile, although she wasn't so sure about Will moving to stand beside her and rest his hand on her shoulder.

She should be angry at being ambushed this way, but how could she be?

So she told herself it might be the last time they were together and allowed herself to indulge in all the wonderful feelings a simple touch on her shoulder could produce.

Charlotte was obviously entranced by the bird, who was tugging at her hair and hopping on her head.

'Look, Daddy, look at him.'

'Let's go outside and watch the river,' Will suggested, and Alex recovered enough from the unexpectedness of the visit to find some biscuits in the pantry and cheese from the fridge.

Will produced a couple of bottles of light beer from the bag he'd carried in.

'You did say you liked beer, didn't you?' he checked, and Alex could only smile.

She took the measly plate of snacks out onto the deck then squatted down to talk to Charlotte.

'I'm Alex,' she said.

'I know, Daddy told me,' the very confident young lady said. 'And he told me about the river and that you've got a boat. Can we go out on the boat?'

'It's getting a bit late for boating,' Alex said, wishing she could add that they'd go another day but not wanting to make false promises to a child.

Particularly this child!

Buddy had fluttered onto the railing and Charlotte, done with her conversation with her hostess, followed.

'Oh, you've got a beach. I like beaches. Can I play on your beach?'

This time Will came to Alex's rescue.

'I think it's a bit late and getting a bit cold for playing on the beach, poppet,' he said, 'but I brought the bag of toys you take when you go visiting. Perhaps you'd like to show them to Buddy.'

Overcome by the unexpectedness of it all, Alex sank down into a chair, watching the little girl pull a zoo of soft stuffed animals out of a bag, holding each one up for Buddy's inspection before placing it carefully in a row on the edge of the deck.

The simple scene made Alex's heart ache for what might have been—the family she'd been foolish enough to allow herself to dream of.

'Okay, here's the beer, and here's the list.'

Will sat beside her, setting her beer on the table and pulling out the list.

'The ones marked with an R are people Robyn knows and she's going to contact them. You and I are going to search out the rest. We'll start with the ones at the bottom. These are people Robyn remembered from school—older sisters of her friends. She says she knew about the touching and, because she was younger, she must have heard it from someone.'

There were six names and someone, possibly Robyn, had added phone numbers of the ex-students' parents.

Alex looked at the man who was doing all this for her—looked at the man she loved—but the despair she'd been feeling all day had only intensified.

'What good would it do?' she asked. 'It's too late now—the story is out there.'

'That's why we have to get every bit of evidence we can to refute it, and once that's done, the paper will print a retraction,' Will growled. 'And soon!'

Alex shook her head, but he wasn't having any of it, reaching out to put his arm around her shoulders, pulling her towards him as he said quietly, 'Alex, you gave me the greatest gift of all, the strength to love again. So now, my love, I'm asking you—begging you—to take some of my strength, and fight this with me.'

She looked into his eyes, intense with feeling, and the 'love' word hung between them.

He was right!

It was time to fight back.

'I'll just get my mobile,' she said, and slipped into the kitchen, returning with a smile as she watched Buddy dancing around the stuffed toys, Charlotte clapping her hands in delight.

Moving a little away from the child, she phoned the first number on the list. Wilson, she remembered the name.

Her heart jittered around in her chest as she considered the reaction of whoever answered when she said *her* name, but her voice only quivered slightly when she responded to a 'Hello'.

'Mrs Wilson, this is Alex Hudson, and I was trying to get in touch with...' she glanced at the list '...Barbara.'

'Oh, Alex, how good to hear your voice. I wanted to

phone to say I knew it was a lie. He didn't rape Barbara but he did touch her a lot. She didn't tell me until after the Spencers had left town, so I couldn't help you at the trial, but I've talked to other people and the man was a monster.'

Alex tried to speak but couldn't, the lump in her throat too big to let air through. Seeing her predicament—and probably the tears streaming down her cheeks—Will took the phone and introduced himself. Yes, he was the doctor from the ICU, yes, he remembered Mr Wilson being in. How was he?

But eventually he got the conversation back on track.

'I knew Alex back then, Mrs Wilson. She lived next door with two doctors from the hospital who believed her story completely, as my family did. But ever since she came home to see her father again, she's been a target of a stalker—phone calls, a rock through her window, nasty things spray-painted on her house. This is obviously the work of the same person and we're trying to find out anything we can about what was going on at the school and church at that time.'

Silence on this end of the phone as Mrs Wilson poured out all she knew to Will, Alex having recovered now and wondering what on earth could be taking so long.

Then Will talking again.

'Thank you, Mrs Wilson, that would be a great help. The more people who are willing to write to the paper, telling what they knew of the man, the better. Alex is a wonderful doctor and it's wrong that she should be driven out of town like this.'

More silence then, 'No, you're right, we won't let it happen.'

He put down the phone, and put out his hand for a high five.

Alex responded although it seemed a little premature to be high-fiving.

'Well?'

Will settled back beside her and took her hand, cold and slightly damp from the beer glass.

'Mrs Wilson says that her daughter told her there was a rumour he was having an affair with one of the students. If that was the case, maybe he'd told the girl he'd marry her. Given that he left town almost straight after the trial, it might have given that girl—or woman now—reason to think you'd ruined her life.'

'Oh, dear, how desperately sad,' Alex said.

Will frowned at her.

'For who?' he asked.

Alex turned towards him. 'For the girl, of course. You can bet if he didn't rape her to begin the affair, he seduced her into sex, then just used her. Maybe she was getting older than he liked and he turned to me.'

She shuddered and Will put his arm around her again.

'Let's eat before we do any more. Charlotte will have some food then promptly fall asleep. I assume you don't mind if we put her on the couch until we're finished here and I can take her home.'

'Of course not,' Alex told him, turning to watch his daughter still entertaining the bird. 'She is such a sweetie!'

The sadness in Alex's voice meant Will had to give her another hug, before getting up to heat and serve the takeaway he'd brought.

They ate at the table, Buddy behaving himself for once, and when the meal was over, Charlotte yawned.

'Are we going home, Daddy?'

Will picked her up.

'How about we stay a little longer?' he said. 'I'll take

you upstairs to have a wash and then you can have a sleep on Alex's couch while Daddy finishes some business.'

'Okay,' his daughter said sleepily, and Will blessed the fact that she'd always been a good sleeper. Playing flat out one minute then asleep the next.

'But I'll want my animals, and can Buddy come in while I sleep?

'I'm sure he can, but he mightn't stay there. Although maybe he's ready for a sleep too, and we can put his cage in near you.'

Alex was happy to put Buddy to bed in his cage, and Will moved the cage into the living room so Charlotte could turn her sleepy eyes towards her new friend.

Will put his arm around Alex's shoulder and together they watched the child fall asleep, Buddy obviously realising he had a serious job and refraining from comment.

They were walking back to the deck when Will's phone rang. Praying he wasn't needed at work, he checked the screen—not work—and answered.

And listened.

And listened.

Alex returned to the deck and waited. She'd failed in her first attempt at a phone call, so what else was there to do?

Think about the situation, that's what, her head suggested, but Will and Charlotte's visit had brought her such happiness she couldn't be angry about it.

He finally joined her, a huge smile on his face.

'Well, Mrs Wilson's story is borne out. That last call was Robyn who's heard it from three different sources—this talk of a secret affair.'

Alex shook her head in disbelief.

'And no one knew?'

'Someone must have,' Will said. 'Or at least suspected.'

Another phone ringing, this time the landline. Fortunately, Alex had carried the handset out onto the deck so that if anyone did ring, it wouldn't wake Charlotte.

Lifting it, she said a very tentative hello, then heard the familiar voice on the other end, a voice that had changed very little in twenty years.

'Caitlin, I can't believe this. How are you? Where are you?'

She listened as her old best friend explained she was living in Sydney, then added, 'But for some mad reason, I always check out the local paper on the internet.'

There was a pause before she added, 'Well, it isn't an unknown reason at all, Chrissie is a reporter for it.'

Alex remembered Caitlin's older sister. She'd been pretty and very popular at the church.

And? Alex wanted to add, but something held her back, some instinct that said Caitlin had more to say.

'I'm so sorry, Alex,' she finally continued. 'I know I should have said something at the time but my parents—well, they don't speak to me any more because I even suggested such a thing—but Chrissie was having an affair with Spencer. It had been going on for a couple of years—from when she was sixteen, like you were. I didn't know for sure until after he left town and Chrissie turned on me because my friend had ruined her life for ever. She ranted on like a madwoman, going on about how he had promised to divorce his wife and marry her and how she wanted to have his babies—awful stuff!'

'Oh, Caitlin, I'm so sorry,' was all Alex could manage.

'You're sorry?' Caitlin all but shouted the words. 'How do you think I feel that my sister has done this to you? She's probably sleeping with the newspaper editor now to get him to print such scurrilous stuff. I'm going to get a retraction, make her tell the whole story.'

'Calm down,' Alex said, smiling as she remembered the young Caitlin firing up over injustices. 'I know what she's done was unforgiveable, but if you think back to how young she was and how much it must have scarred her—let's see if we can sort it out without hurting her even more. She's a victim too.'

'Well, you're a nicer person than I am,' Caitlin said, 'but keep in touch and let me know what I *can* do.'

Alex wrote down the phone number Caitlin gave her, and promised to keep in touch.

'Found your old friend?' Will said, smiling at her as she looked up from the phone.

'Yes,' she said soberly, 'and my stalker.' She explained about Caitlin's sister, and her job as a reporter on the local paper.

Will reached out and touched her shoulder, kneading at it and running his fingers along her neck.

'But you're not going to use that, are you?' he said, and Alex smiled up at him.

'How could I?' she said. 'Do you really think a six-teen-year-old schoolgirl would have seduced him? Do you think he didn't pick her out and groom her until he knew she was ready? What he did to her has already cast a huge shadow over her life. I can't hurt her any more.'

'So,' said Will, 'we go back to the lists and get as many people as possible to write letters to the paper, naming Spencer, the women telling of the times he touched them when they were young, others explaining how their strict church upbringing meant they couldn't come forward at the trial.'

He pulled her to her feet and held her in his arms.

'We'll beat this,' he said. 'Just you wait and see!'

* * *

The media storm that followed the newspaper article was beyond anything Alex could ever have imagined. Somehow, in far-off America, the Armitages had heard of it, and a letter signed by both of them appeared in the paper.

But what affected Alex most was the number of women who came forward to say he'd behaved improperly towards them, one even admitting he'd raped her but she'd been too afraid to come forward.

They all praised Alex for speaking out when she had and so warning him against trying it again on other teenage girls.

And all sent regrets that not only had the wrong verdict been reached but that the case had once again become public.

'Which still leaves us with Chrissie,' Will said to her one evening, some weeks later, when, as had become a custom, Charlotte was asleep on the couch and they were sitting on the deck.

'I think I need to speak to her myself,' Alex said. 'I don't want to hand her in to the police, but I do want her to know that I know it was her.'

'I'll come with you—you have no idea what she could do. She could be more incensed than ever.'

Alex smiled at her protector.

'No, Will, it's something I have to do alone. I'll meet her in a public place—a coffee shop. Nothing can happen there.'

And nothing did, apart from tears and apologies and the outpouring of a grief that had been so deep for Chrissie it had escalated to a kind of madness.

'I hadn't thought about Mr Spencer for years. I'd buried all thoughts of that time,' Chrissie said through her tears. 'But when I found out that you were back in town all my anger came flooding back. Something inside me just…snapped.'

'Have you thought about getting counselling?' Alex suggested gently. 'I could get some referrals from the hospital for you.'

'Caitlin's been on to me about counselling,' Chrissie said.

'It can be very helpful,' Alex said softly. 'I should know—I saw a counsellor for years.'

Her tears spent, Chrissie managed a watery smile. 'It's a bit late, but I know I need it.'

'It's never too late,' Alex said. 'I'm only just beginning to realise that myself.' She reached across the table and took Chrissie's hand, prompting another flood of tears.

'I'm so sorry for what I did to you, Alex.' Chrissie sobbed. 'I know you could have exposed me as the girl who had the affair with him. I've been disciplined at work, even though the editor has been delighted with the controversy. Distribution numbers are way up as everyone reads the salacious gossip about a man they once thought was wonderful. I was such a fool.'

She sighed, and more tears slid down her cheeks.

Alex squeezed her fingers.

'It wasn't your fault,' she assured Chrissie. 'It was *never* your fault.'

Promising to get professional help, Chrissie said goodbye.

Emotionally drained, Alex struggled back to the rooms, where Brian Lane insisted he'd take the afternoon patients and do the ward round.

'After all,' he said, 'I'll be gone for good in a couple of weeks. My wife will take that long to pack up the kids

and the house, and I want to see each and every one of
our patients so they know you have my full support.'

He smiled at Alex, then added, 'Not that most of them
need it. The way the phone's been ringing, I might regret
leaving the practice.'

Alex thanked him and departed, driving slowly home,
enjoying the ferry journey.

Friday, and Will was off duty so he and Charlotte were
coming to stay over so they could go out on the river early
in the morning, before it got too hot.

Alex had been very uncertain about this arrange-
ment, but when they'd talked to Charlotte about it and
showed her Alex's old room, where she would sleep, she'd
asked, 'But where will you sleep, Daddy? Will Alex let
you sleep in her bed? Because that room's nicer than the
other room.'

'It's as if she's blessed us,' Will had said, and Alex
knew he was probably right.

They came at dusk, Will laden down as ever with bags
of toys and clothing.

But this time Alex had cooked dinner for them, spa-
ghetti and meatballs at Charlotte's request.

With Buddy on her shoulder and tweaking at her hair,
the little girl played happily on the deck while Alex finished the dinner and Will made a salad to go with it.

Charlotte ate and immediately asked to go to bed.

'But with Buddy in his cage as well,' she insisted.

Finally alone, they stood on the deck, looking at the river,
silvered by the light of the moon.

'Have I ever mentioned that I love you?' Will murmured, kissing Alex on the temple.

'Not often enough,' Alex whispered, leaning into him
and turning so his lips could meet her mouth.

The kiss was different, not a prelude to passion, as so many of their kisses had become, but more a declaration of the love they shared and a promise of what was to come.

Together they had faced the pain of the accusations against Alex and come through it, their love stronger for being forged in devastation.

Slowly, they made their way upstairs, opening the gate at the top that Will had installed to keep Charlotte safe. They stopped at the door of Alex's old room and looked at the sleeping child, Buddy in his cage on the desk at the end of the bed and Alex's old toy galah clasped in her hands.

'She's a precious gift,' Alex whispered. 'Thank you for sharing her with me.'

'You're the gift, to both of us,' he countered. 'You gave me back the gift of love.'

They made love quietly, ever aware of the sleeping child just down the hall, and Alex fell asleep with her hand on Will's shoulder, secure, for the first time, in a relationship.

A relationship that exceeded all her dreams.

EPILOGUE

ALEX COLLECTED CHARLOTTE from kindergarten, laughing as the little girl hugged her around the legs.

'That baby's taking up too much room and I can't hug you properly,' Charlotte complained.

'But not for much longer,' Alex promised her. 'One more week, that's all you have to wait.'

The dark eyes, so like Will's, looked up at her.

'And you really will let me help look after him?'

'Or her,' Alex reminded Charlotte. They'd decided not to know the sex of the child she carried for all Charlotte was convinced it would be a boy.

'And, yes,' Alex added, 'we'll need you to help. When the baby's out on the deck in his pram, you'll have to keep Buddy from bouncing on him and waking him up.'

'I can do that easily. Buddy loves me,' Charlotte declared, as Alex fastened her into her car seat.

And Buddy did indeed love the little girl who'd come to live with them. He was her constant companion when she was at home, and even greeted her before he greeted Alex when the pair of them came in together.

'And we'll call him Bob.' Charlotte wasn't finished with the baby conversation and her favourite television character was named Bob.

'We'll see,' Alex responded, glad Charlotte wasn't

old enough to understand a parental 'We'll see' often meant no.

Or even 'No way'.

'So how's my family?' Will asked, coming out of the house to greet the pair.

'What are you doing home?'

Alex's question was lost in Charlotte's cries of delight as she flung herself into his arms.

'I thought my wife stopping work, even if it's only for a few months, was a special enough occasion to deserve a celebration so I skived off, leaving Josh in charge, and cooked our dinner. You sit out on the deck and put your feet up, and I'll bring you a small libation of French champagne.'

'French yet!' Alex teased, finally getting her turn in her husband's arms.

But she was happy to sit on the deck and put her feet up. There'd be little time to rest after the baby arrived. She'd taken three months' maternity leave then Will would take the next three months off work, so the baby would have a parent at home all the time.

After that a nanny would come two days a week, with both Alex and Will working alternate short weeks.

Alex looked out at the river and sighed.

In theory it sounded good, but would it work?

'You're worrying again,' Will scolded, as he brought out their drinks, the champagne cooling in her parents' ice bucket.

She touched the side of it, thinking back, remembering her parents in happier times, aware that all the pain and bitterness she'd felt had vanished through the power of love.

Will's love!

And the smile of a little girl who already called her Mummy...

'Happy?' Will asked, as he sat down beside her and took her hand.

'There should be a better word,' Alex said, smiling as Charlotte and Buddy joined them, both having sensed there might be biscuits on the table.

'We're calling the baby Bob,' Charlotte announced to her father.

Will raised one quizzical eyebrow at Alex.

'This too shall pass,' she said. 'We know that now. With the love we share we're strong enough to cope with anything. Even a little girl called Bob...'

* * * * *

MILLS & BOON®
Hardback – May 2015

ROMANCE

The Sheikh's Secret Babies	Lynne Graham
The Sins of Sebastian Rey-Defoe	Kim Lawrence
At Her Boss's Pleasure	Cathy Williams
Captive of Kadar	Trish Morey
The Marakaios Marriage	Kate Hewitt
Craving Her Enemy's Touch	Rachael Thomas
The Greek's Pregnant Bride	Michelle Smart
Greek's Last Redemption	Caitlin Crews
The Pregnancy Secret	Cara Colter
A Bride for the Runaway Groom	Scarlet Wilson
The Wedding Planner and the CEO	Alison Roberts
Bound by a Baby Bump	Ellie Darkins
Always the Midwife	Alison Roberts
Midwife's Baby Bump	Susanne Hampton
A Kiss to Melt Her Heart	Emily Forbes
Tempted by Her Italian Surgeon	Louisa George
Daring to Date Her Ex	Annie Claydon
The One Man to Heal Her	Meredith Webber
The Sheikh's Pregnancy Proposal	Fiona Brand
Minding Her Boss's Business	Janice Maynard

0415 GEN STD HB

MILLS & BOON®
Large Print – May 2015

ROMANCE

The Secret His Mistress Carried	Lynne Graham
Nine Months to Redeem Him	Jennie Lucas
Fonseca's Fury	Abby Green
The Russian's Ultimatum	Michelle Smart
To Sin with the Tycoon	Cathy Williams
The Last Heir of Monterrato	Andie Brock
Inherited by Her Enemy	Sara Craven
Taming the French Tycoon	Rebecca Winters
His Very Convenient Bride	Sophie Pembroke
The Heir's Unexpected Return	Jackie Braun
The Prince She Never Forgot	Scarlet Wilson

HISTORICAL

Marriage Made in Money	Sophia James
Chosen by the Lieutenant	Anne Herries
Playing the Rake's Game	Bronwyn Scott
Caught in Scandal's Storm	Helen Dickson
Bride for a Knight	Margaret Moore

MEDICAL

Playing the Playboy's Sweetheart	Carol Marinelli
Unwrapping Her Italian Doc	Carol Marinelli
A Doctor by Day...	Emily Forbes
Tamed by the Renegade	Emily Forbes
A Little Christmas Magic	Alison Roberts
Christmas with the Maverick Millionaire	Scarlet Wilson

MILLS & BOON®
Hardback – June 2015

ROMANCE

The Bride Fonseca Needs	Abby Green
Sheikh's Forbidden Conquest	Chantelle Shaw
Protecting the Desert Heir	Caitlin Crews
Seduced into the Greek's World	Dani Collins
Tempted by Her Billionaire Boss	Jennifer Hayward
Married for the Prince's Convenience	Maya Blake
The Sicilian's Surprise Wife	Tara Pammi
Russian's Ruthless Demand	Michelle Conder
His Unexpected Baby Bombshell	Soraya Lane
Falling for the Bridesmaid	Sophie Pembroke
A Millionaire for Cinderella	Barbara Wallace
From Paradise...to Pregnant!	Kandy Shepherd
Midwife...to Mum!	Sue MacKay
His Best Friend's Baby	Susan Carlisle
Italian Surgeon to the Stars	Melanie Milburne
Her Greek Doctor's Proposal	Robin Gianna
New York Doc to Blushing Bride	Janice Lynn
Still Married to Her Ex!	Lucy Clark
The Sheikh's Secret Heir	Kristi Gold
Carrying A King's Child	Katherine Garbera

MILLS & BOON®
Large Print – June 2015

ROMANCE

The Redemption of Darius Sterne	Carole Mortimer
The Sultan's Harem Bride	Annie West
Playing by the Greek's Rules	Sarah Morgan
Innocent in His Diamonds	Maya Blake
To Wear His Ring Again	Chantelle Shaw
The Man to Be Reckoned With	Tara Pammi
Claimed by the Sheikh	Rachael Thomas
Her Brooding Italian Boss	Susan Meier
The Heiress's Secret Baby	Jessica Gilmore
A Pregnancy, a Party & a Proposal	Teresa Carpenter
Best Friend to Wife and Mother?	Caroline Anderson

HISTORICAL

The Lost Gentleman	Margaret McPhee
Breaking the Rake's Rules	Bronwyn Scott
Secrets Behind Locked Doors	Laura Martin
Taming His Viking Woman	Michelle Styles
The Knight's Broken Promise	Nicole Locke

MEDICAL

Midwife's Christmas Proposal	Fiona McArthur
Midwife's Mistletoe Baby	Fiona McArthur
A Baby on Her Christmas List	Louisa George
A Family This Christmas	Sue MacKay
Falling for Dr December	Susanne Hampton
Snowbound with the Surgeon	Annie Claydon

MILLS & BOON®

Why shop at millsandboon.co.uk?

Each year, thousands of romance readers find their perfect read at millsandboon.co.uk. That's because we're passionate about bringing you the very best romantic fiction. Here are some of the advantages of shopping at www.millsandboon.co.uk:

* **Get new books first**—you'll be able to buy your favourite books one month before they hit the shops

* **Get exclusive discounts**—you'll also be able to buy our specially created monthly collections, with up to 50% off the RRP

* **Find your favourite authors**—latest news, interviews and new releases for all your favourite authors and series on our website, plus ideas for what to try next

* **Join in**—once you've bought your favourite books, don't forget to register with us to rate, review and join in the discussions

Visit **www.millsandboon.co.uk**
for all this and more today!